"You didn't find the wrong man, Selby, and you know it."

She flushed scarlet. "I know nothing of the kind. And while we're on the subject, what did you tell your parents? Your father keeps looking at me as if I'm going to make off with the family silver, and your mother seems to think we're about to elope."

"Ah, well. Dad's a lawyer—cautious."

"That doesn't explain your mother."

"*Nothing* explains my mother," he told her cheerfully.

Selby looked stern. "You must have said *something*."

"All I said was that I'd met a charming, nutty girl, and that I'd fallen in love with her," he said calmly.

She was assailed by a savage joy, which was instantly replaced by panic. "You can't be. You don't know me."

Celia Scott, originally from England, came to Canada for a vacation and began an "instant love affair" with the country. She started out in acting but liked romance fiction and was encouraged to make writing it her career when her husband gave her a typewriter as a wedding present. She now finds writing infinitely more creative than acting since she gets to act out all her characters' roles, and direct, too.

Books by Celia Scott

RELATIVE ATTRACTION
Celia Scott

Harlequin Books

TORONTO • NEW YORK • LONDON
AMSTERDAM • PARIS • SYDNEY • HAMBURG
STOCKHOLM • ATHENS • TOKYO • MILAN
MADRID • WARSAW • BUDAPEST • AUCKLAND

ISBN 0-373-03306-0

RELATIVE ATTRACTION

CHAPTER ONE

"WE'VE LANDED. You can stop flying the plane, love," said the woman in the next seat.

Selby's knuckles unclenched and she sagged back in her seat.

"It must be awful making a transatlantic flight when you're scared of flying," the woman sympathized.

"Oh! I'm not scared of flying, it's just the coming down I don't like," said Selby. "I'm not wild about going up, either," she added with a grin.

She had an infectious smile, and the woman in the next seat smiled back, pleased she'd been seated next to such a pleasant young woman for the flight. "At least you didn't get airsick," she said, and launched into a detailed account of a relative of hers who had become so airsick that the pilot had arranged for an ambulance to meet the plane when it landed.

Selby tuned out. People were always willing to talk to her, and in her job as a journalist for a women's magazine this was usually an asset, but right now she had other things on her mind, like finding the Halifax address the detective had given her.

Passengers started to stand up and stretch, opening overhead compartments and pulling down coats and bags of duty-free items.

"... and then she had to be hospitalized for a week on top of that. Some holiday!" the woman concluded. She patted Selby's arm. "Doesn't apply to you, of course, love. You'll have a wonderful time in Halifax. September's a lovely month for a visit. You did say it was your first visit to Canada, didn't you?"

Selby nodded and took a mirror out of her bag. "Ugh!" she said.

"You've got nothing to complain about," said the woman. "You look as fresh and pretty as you did when we boarded."

"I don't feel either," Selby replied wryly. "I feel like an old cushion."

It was true there were smudges of fatigue beneath her gray eyes, and she was so pale the dusting of freckles over her nose was more noticeable than usual. But she was still a startlingly pretty girl.

She rubbed a trace of blusher onto her cheeks and ran a comb through her short brown curls. She might be grieving inside, but no one would guess it. Her grandmother had always said, "We're not the type to look like dying swans, lovey. We wind up looking like dying ducks."

Selby's eyes suddenly stung with tears and she blinked furiously, willing herself not to think of Maisy; not now, not when she was too tired to keep herself in check.

"Are you going to be doing any traveling while you're in Canada?" asked her seatmate, reaching down for her flight bag.

"I'm not sure." She might be. If he wasn't at that address, she would have to search further.

"Well there's plenty to see in Halifax. If you get the chance, you should visit Uniacke House. It's a lovely spot."

"I'll remember," promised Selby, reaching for her jacket.

The woman heaved her bag onto her lap. "Although I seem to remember you telling me at Heathrow this was a business trip."

"Partly business." And that was partly true. Her editor had suggested she might want to make this a working holiday. Selby was clever at finding human-interest stories wherever she went, and her editor had thought a bit of work on her leave might help take her mind off her bereavement. What she hadn't known was that this journey was not a holiday but a vendetta. An attempt to right a long-overdue wrong.

The woman swung herself into the crowded aisle. "Well, you have a lovely time, dear. I hope the weather holds." She nodded at the morning sun glinting off the wings of the plane. "It might not be warm enough for swimming, but the beaches are still nice in this weather."

At the luggage carousel, fatigue hit Selby like a mallet. Suddenly all she wanted was a bath and bed. A healthy girl, she didn't usually have trouble sleeping, but since her grandmother's death she had spent a lot of time lying awake, staring into the dark and going over and over what Maisy had told her during those last weeks.

Selby had come to Canada on impulse, but this was nothing new. She was a creature of sudden impulses and hasty actions.

The decision to embark on this personal crusade was made in the space of a minute. She hadn't been able to sleep, brooding about Maisy, burning with anger at the injustice of it all. Recognizing sleep would never come at this rate, she had got up and made herself a cup of cocoa, and had stayed in the kitchen of the shared flat to drink it. There it had come to her in a flash that the best way to use the money from the sale of Maisy's house was to go to Canada and find out if... if *that man* was still alive and, if he was, to confront him.

She had been brought up by her grandmother, and now Maisy was gone, leaving a gaping hole in Selby's world. Selby wanted to do something, *had* to do something, no matter how foolish it might seem to others, to avenge her beloved grandmother.

Maisy had lost her man in the Second World War, and Selby's mother, Danielle, had been her only child. Danielle had been the apple of Maisy's eye. She was pretty and bright, with a warm and loving heart, and although Maisy hadn't had an easy time bringing up her daughter on her own, the two of them had been happy together. Danielle had married a man Maisy liked, and the young couple had started their own business.

Life had been good. The business thrived and after a couple of years Selby arrived. The little family was content. Danielle and her husband hadn't taken a holiday since their honeymoon, so Maisy had nagged them into taking a coach tour through Italy. The third day of the tour the coach was in an accident, and Danielle and her husband were killed.

Selby had been two at the time. She had no conscious memory of the tragedy, but she did remember Maisy's tears when, years later, she'd found a worn postcard in her grandmother's sewing box: "Dear Mum, thanks again for suggesting this tour. Geoff says the spaghetti here isn't a patch on yours! A kiss for you and Selby. Love."

The card was signed "D & G."

For years Maisy blamed herself for sending them on that holiday.

SELBY CHECKED into her hotel, went up to her room and took a leisurely bath, then she drew the blinds and lay on the bed. Today she didn't toss and turn, for she was too tired. Besides, she had nothing to brood about now—she was doing something positive for Maisy. She fell at once into a sound sleep.

She awoke a few hours later and quickly showered before going out for a walk before dinner.

She asked the clerk on the front desk for a map of the city. "You should go to the Public Gardens," he said. "They're really nice."

"I'll do that," she said, smiling, although sightseeing was not on her list of activities.

It was a pleasant, warm evening, and if she hadn't been suffering from jet lag, she would have thoroughly enjoyed strolling through the gently sloping streets lined with attractive old houses. As it was, she was too keyed up about her plan to pay much attention to the scenery.

She ate baked bluefish in a restaurant on the waterfront, and then as she sipped her coffee she pored over a map of Halifax. Before she'd left the hotel, she'd looked up D. Forest in the phone book, half expecting to be disappointed, but there it was, and the address matched the one the private detective had given her. The area was called the North West Arm, and the tourist information on the back of the map described it as "a magnificent four-kilometer fjordlike arm of the sea, lined with exclusive homes."

"Bastard!" muttered Selby, remembering her grandmother's modest little house. "Lying, cheating bastard."

The waitress offered more coffee, but she refused. More coffee would keep her awake, and she wanted a good night's sleep, for tomorrow she needed a clear head. Tomorrow she had a score to settle.

The following morning she awoke edgy with tension and forced herself to take a long bath. Normally she hardly bothered with makeup, but this morning she took her time, applying eye shadow and mascara, outlining her full lips with coral lipstick. She didn't want Daniel Forest thinking she was some deadbeat arriving at his "exclusive home" to beg for charity. She didn't want charity. She wanted an admission of guilt.

She smoothed the miniskirt of her new emerald wool suit over her slender hips and pinned a small antique brooch at the neck of her blouse. It was rather a prim touch, but the brooch had belonged to her grandmother, and she felt it would bring her luck.

"I'll make him sorry, Gran," she whispered to her reflection. "It won't all have been for nothing." And checking her purse to make sure she had the necessary documents of proof—the birth and death certificates, the photographs—she set her soft mouth in an unusually grim line and went down to find a taxi.

They hadn't been kidding in the tourist brochure—the homes on the North West Arm *were* exclusive. And Daniel Forest's home was by far the most exclusive of the lot. The taxi swept up a tree-shaded drive flanked by flower beds that would have done justice to the public gardens. She caught a glimpse of velvet lawn running down to the water's edge, where a couple of sailboats and a motor launch rocked gently at their moorings. These symbols of affluence fueled her righteous indignation even more, and her expression grew grimmer.

She rang the bell and stood, one neatly shod foot tapping the brick step. Her face, reflected in the highly polished brass knocker, was distorted like the reflection in an amusement-park mirror, but this was no outing to an amusement park. This was the time of reckoning.

The door was opened by an elderly woman wearing an apron over a dark uniform. A housekeeper possibly, not a member of the family, that much was certain.

"Yes, miss?" She was not unfriendly, but she didn't roll out the welcome mat, either.

"I'm...er..." Now that she was so close to her quarry, Selby had difficulty making her voice work properly. "I'm looking for...for Mr. Daniel Forest. Have I come to the right address?"

"I guess so," said the woman cautiously.

"Then I'd like to see him, please."

"I'm sorry." She sounded firm. "That's not possible."

"I must see him," said Selby, sounding equally firm. 'I've come all the way from England to see him."

"It's not possible to see Mr. Forest because he's away," the woman said.

"Then I'll wait till he gets back," said Selby. The woman gave her a wintry smile. "You'll have to wait a long time. He's in Europe."

"In *Europe!*" Selby's voice rose to an undignified squeak. It had never occurred to her that he might be away.

"They'll be back in ten days. You could come back then." She started to close the door.

"Wait!" Selby cried, "Where in Europe?" If he was in England, she could track him down there.

"The family's traveling around. I'm not sure where they are. You'd better come back later."

She could come back in ten days, for she'd still be in Canada, but she felt as deflated as a balloon with a pin in it.

"Oh, well, I'll have to, I suppose," she said.

"Who shall I tell him called?" the woman asked.

"He wouldn't know my name."

No, not mine. God knows if he'll remember Maisy's, but I'll jog his memory for him. I'll jog it hard!

She said, "I'll come back in ten days, then," and started to walk down the path when the woman called after her.

"Just a minute, miss! I'm not thinking straight. Is it Mr. *Danny* you're wanting?"

Selby stopped in midstride. "Danny Forest—that's right." Danny was the name her grandmother had used.

"Well, why didn't you say so? He's in Newfoundland. In his lighthouse."

"His *lighthouse?*" Selby returned to the front door. "You did say lighthouse?"

"Yes, but..." The woman hesitated, looking uneasy.

"If you'd give me the address?"

"I'm not sure. He...he doesn't encourage visitors."

"But I've come all the way from England." Selby smiled warmly and the woman looked less uncertain. "It would be so sad if I had to go back again without seeing Mr.... Mr. Danny. I wouldn't take up much of his time. I just want to see him for a few minutes."

"Newfoundland's rather a long way to go for a few minutes."

"But I've got a very important message for him. From someone...he used to know," said Selby, her luminous eyes innocently wide.

Selby's grandmother had always maintained that Selby could charm a cat into taking swimming lessons if she put her mind to it. "Come into the hall," said the woman now. "I'll write the address down for you."

She held the door open and Selby stepped inside. The scent of floor polish and roses greeted her, white paint sparkled, silver gleamed. Danny Forest seemed to have done well for himself since 1942.

The woman took a leather book from the drawer of a satinwood desk and scribbled an address on a piece of paper. "The phone number's unlisted, and it's more than my life's worth to give it to you," she said, "but you could write to him there."

"Yes, I could," replied Selby, squinting down at the piece of paper. "Wreck Cove Light, Savage Harbour, Newfoundland." It didn't sound exactly cozy, but she'd go there even if it was the end of the earth.

"I hope I've done the right thing," the woman said as Selby was leaving, "but seeing that you've come all the way from England . . ." She looked doubtful.

"You've saved me a wasted journey," said Selby, "I shan't forget it." Danny Forest wouldn't forget it, either, she vowed silently.

When she reached the road, she turned to look back at the house. The housekeeper was still standing in the doorway—looking worried.

THREE DAYS LATER Selby drove into Savage Harbour. She couldn't believe it had taken her so long. What had started as a simple trip had turned into the kind of nightmare she got when she ate too much rich food and dreamed she was hopelessly lost, incapable of turning back or waking up.

First, the flight to St. John's had been delayed because of fog in Newfoundland. Then, when she'd arrived, the rental car she'd ordered in Halifax wasn't available. No one seemed particulary concerned about it until Selby lost her temper and insisted the manager give her a car that had been reserved for somebody else.

She drove out of St. John's still tingling with rage only to discover that her problems were just beginning. The fog closed in again, she couldn't find Savage Harbour on her map, and the few people she passed seemed never to have heard of it. She spent her first night in a miserable motel miles out of her way, fog swirling outside the window, with a packet of crackers and an apple she'd bought in case of an emergency for her supper.

When she finally arrived at Savage Harbour at noon the next day, she felt as if she'd been on the road for weeks. The fog had lifted so that it hovered like a metallic lid over the tiny village, which consisted of a huddle of cottages, a small pebble beach and a post office that also served as both general store and restaurant. On one side of the beach granite cliffs reared up into the grayness, and on the other the rocks formed a craggy headland, at the end of which she could just make out the shape of a lighthouse.

By this time Selby had jumped to so many conclusions she was dizzy. The idea that Danny Forest lived in a lighthouse at all puzzled and intrigued her. Her grandmother had never mentioned anything about lighthouses, and he couldn't be a lighthouse keeper because she remembered reading somewhere that lighthouses were automatic these days. So the lighthouse must be his summer residence. But why take up summer residence on a barren outcrop of rock when you owned a beautiful house and garden within driving distance of some of the loveliest scenery imaginable? She decided he was simply a certifiable nut case and, remembering his housekeeper's apprehension, a bad-tempered one to boot, which meant that Danny Forest was most likely a bully, as well as a cheat.

She parked her car and went into the general store. It was warm and smelled of bacon and coffee and paraffin, with a whiff of fish for added effect. A small heater stood on top of a potbellied stove, creating a circle of warmth, a nice contrast to the general dankness. There was also a counter with four stools in front of it, a plate of bran muffins covered with a glass dome and a pot of coffee on a hot plate.

There was no one around. Ducking beneath a cluster of oilskins that hung from the ceiling like stalactites, Selby went to a door at the back and opened it, revealing a small parlor. From beneath her feet came the sound of metal hitting metal, followed by a muffled oath.

She went over to an open door with steps leading to the basement and called, "Hello!"

There was another clang, then a woman's voice muttered, "Dang and blast!"

"Hello," Selby called again. "Hello!"

"I hear you, but I'm trying to fix this blasted boiler," the voice said, "and I can't be in two places at the same time."

"I want to buy coffee and a muffin," Selby shouted.

"Help yourself. There's cream and sugar on the counter. I'll be up in a bit."

Selby went behind the counter and poured coffee into one of the thick mugs she found draining beside the sink. She took a muffin and bit into it. It was delicious. She finished it and took another one, polishing it off in record time, then, holding her mug of coffee, she wandered around the store to examine the merchandise.

It was a veritable Aladdin's cave: bales of twine nestled against boxes of tinned fruit, rubber boots leaned against a freezer full of lobster and ice cream, an assortment of sweaters and foul-weather gear were draped about, and patent medicines and cheap cosmetics filled a shelf. She picked up a magazine entitled *Your Future in the Stars,* and leafed through to her sign. "Love and luck favorable today," she read. "You make a big impression," Checking the date, she discovered that it was six months earlier.

"You don't want to believe everythin' you read," said a female voice.

The woman had come up from the basement and was leaning against the counter, wiping her hands on an oily rag. She was in her late thirties, a large, untidy woman dressed in denim overalls. She surveyed Selby calmly.

"The muffins were delicious. I had two," Selby told her.

"They generally goes fast," said the woman. "You was lucky there was any left. When my husband's around, a dozen goes in as many minutes. But he's driven into Seal Cove to visit his brother, so he didn't get his mitts on 'em." She pitched the rag into a bin. "You visitin' someone or just passin' through?"

"A bit of both," said Selby. She hoisted herself onto a stool. "Could I buy a sandwich, do you think?"

"Buy a full-course dinner if you want, so long as you don't mind crab," said the woman.

"Right now a sandwich would be fine."

"More coffee? The name's Lori, by the way. Lori Pyecroft."

"More coffee would be great. Mine's Selby Maitland." She liked this woman. It wasn't difficult. Like all the islanders she'd met so far, Lori was friendly and easy to like.

"You from away, then?" Lori asked, pouring more coffee into Selby's mug. "Cheese sandwich be okay?"

"Cheese is fine. I drove from St. John's. I got lost."

"You wouldn't be the first one. We don't believe in making it easy for folks to find us." She took a loaf of bread from a bin. "Only got white, okay?"

Nodding, Selby asked, "Don't you like strangers?"

"Oh, we like 'em fine, but good things shouldn't come too easy, right? An' we think Savage Harbour is a pretty good little place."

"It seems to be," said Selby. "Not that I can see much of it in the fog."

"Got to get used to fog if you lives in Newfoundland," said Lori. "You're not from Canada, though, are you? Not with that accent."

"I'm from England. From London."

"Been in Canada long?"

"Four days." It felt much longer. England and Maisy seemed a long time ago. How her grandmother would have enjoyed this trip! She had always relished an adventure. Selby felt a sudden pang of loneliness.

"On vacation, are you?" probed Lori, peeling slices of cheese from a plastic pack.

"I'm looking up some distant friends...." She wavered for a moment. "Er...sort of friends of friends."

Lori shot her a look from under her brows. "That's nice. Do you want scrunchions in your sandwich?"

"Scrunchions?"

"Fried pork fat."

"No, thank you. As a matter of fact," said Selby, "I'm looking for someone called Danny Forest. Do you know him?"

"Sure I know him." She slapped a slice of bread on top of the cheese. "You want to eat it here, or shall I bag it?"

"What?" Selby's pulse had quickened. "Oh! In a bag, please. Do you know where I could find him?"

Lori cut the sandwich in two before replying. "That depends."

"On what?"

"On whether he's out in his boat or not."

"Oh!"

"If he's not, he could still be out collectin'. He does a lot of collectin'." Selby was puzzled. Collecting what, or for what? she wondered. The Red Cross? "Or he could be home." Lori gestured toward the front of the store with her chin. "He lives in the lighthouse."

So, she was in the right place. Tracking him down hadn't been as difficult as she'd feared. Now all that

was left was for her to confront him with the evidence
and watch him squirm.

"Well, I'll try the lighthouse," she said, taking the
paper bag. "How much do I owe you?"

After Lori had given Selby her change, she walked
with her to the front door. "His dory's moored down
near the rocks," she said, pointing toward the headland where Selby could just make out the shape of a
sharp-bowed rowboat moving gently on the swell. "I
guess he decided it's too foggy to be out today."

"I guess so." At this moment he was probably sitting there, secure in his lighthouse, unaware that justice in the form of Selby Maitland had finally run him
to earth. Selby's heart started to beat with anticipa-
tion. "Goodbye," she said to Lori. "It was nice talking to you."

"My pleasure. Always nice to see a new face."

Lori stayed leaning against the door as Selby walked
the narrow path to the lighthouse. When she reached
her destination, Selby turned and waved, but she could
hardly see Lori in the mist, and only the muffled
sound of the shop's bell echoing across the silence told
her Lori had gone back into the store.

The lighthouse looked like a stark white pointer, its
turret wreathed in fog. It was not a welcoming sight.
However, the little front door had been recently
painted a cheerful shade of red, and the knocker, a
fetching brass mermaid, was polished and gleaming.
She applied the mermaid's tail vigorously. The only
thing that happened was a cacophony of hysterical
barking. Then what must have been a large dog hurled

itself against the door like a demented hound from hell.

Startled, she took a step back and called, "Hallo! Is anybody home?" Although how any living creature would be able to hear her over the racket the dog was making was questionable.

She plied the knocker again, and the torrent of barking increased. Either Danny Forest wasn't in, or he was stone-deaf.

She left the front of the lighthouse and walked around to the back. Here, a small window was set into the concrete, and peering through it, she caught a glimpse of some wooden trays, a number of shells, some seaweed and a microscope, before a blond Labrador hurled itself at the glass in a rage.

Hastily she stepped back. Apart from the hysterical dog, the lighthouse seemed to be deserted. Well, she'd just have to wait, and she'd eat her sandwich while she waited, fortifying herself for her meeting with Danny Forest.

There was nowhere to sit, and she'd spent too many hours in the car to enjoy eating her lunch in it, so she decided to go down to the rocks below and see if she could find a suitable spot there.

Slipping and sliding, for the surface was wet from the receding tide, she found a fairly sheltered ledge close to the water, and using her jacket as a cushion, sat down to eat. Today she was dressed in jeans and a thick white sweater, her emerald suit and high-heeled pumps tucked neatly in her suitcase.

Although the fog was clammy, it wasn't really cold, and gradually she started to relax. The sharp cones of barnacles surrounded her and forests of brownish seaweed swayed in the swell of the dark, cold sea. It was if she were alone in the world, enclosed by silvery fog and salt water. At first it was a bit scary, but after a while she began to enjoy the feeling of isolation. There was peace in the sound of the water gently slapping the rocks, and the pungent scent of brine that tickled her nostrils was invigorating. Even the gulls were changed to ghosts materializing out of the dimness and suddenly disappearing again, their cries muffled. Only the mournful bleat of a foghorn broke the stillness.

She finished her lunch, folded the bag and put it in her pocket, then sat, arms wrapped around her knees, gazing hypnotized into the fog.

She should have been devising strategies to use when she confronted her quarry, but she was lulled into a state of suspension and her brain refused to cooperate. It was too nice just sitting on these rocks, taking in nothing more than the rhythmic movement of the sea.

It was then that she noticed a disturbance in the water below her. Something was swimming down there. A seal? Selby loved seals, but she'd never seen one in its natural habitat. What a bonus! She caught her breath with delight.

Whatever it was swam closer to the surface. It was much too big for a seal: it must be a walrus! Did walruses attack people? No, of course they didn't. She was being idiotic. The poor creature was liable to be more frightened of her than the other way around. It might go away if she didn't sit as still as the boulders that surrounded her, and she'd have lost a once-in-a-lifetime chance to observe a walrus close up.

Hardly daring to breathe, she sat immobile. Now she could see a dark shape coming right to the edge of the rock where she was sitting. She clutched her hands more tightly together, and the head and shoulders of a man in scuba-diving gear broke the surface.

Selby gave a little shriek and nearly toppled off her perch.

The man pushed back his mask and stared at her as if she had two heads. "You bloody idiot," he said. "Don't you know the tide's coming in? You could be drowned."

CHAPTER TWO

THIS WAS THE FIRST unfriendly person Selby had met since coming to Newfoundland and she wasn't prepared for it, so instead of telling him to dive back into the sea and stay there, she meekly explained, "I was eating my lunch."

He stared at her in disbelief. His eyes seemed to be the same deep green as the water. "Eating your *lunch?* In this weather?" With one strong movement he swung himself onto the rocks beside her.

Selby stood up. There was something sinister about this dark-clad figure emerging from the sea. She felt safer on her feet. "I'm waiting for somebody," she said.

He gave her another incredulous look. "You have a *date?*" He started removing his flippers. "You have a date on Suicide Rocks?"

"Suicide Rocks!" Now that she looked at them they did seem rather dangerous. "Is that what they're called?"

"As you'll find out if you hang around much longer." He rose to his feet. He was a tall man, lean and hard muscled. "This way," he commanded, picking up his flippers and a mesh bag.

"No, thanks," said Selby, unwilling to follow a complete stranger who had arrived in such an unorthodox fashion and was clad from head to toe in rubber.

"This way," he repeated, grabbing her arm in one large wet hand and dragging her with him.

"Let me go!"

"Look!" He turned her forcibly and she saw that the sea had silently risen behind her, leaving only a small thread of rocks above water.

"Well, there's still a sort of path," she said, shaken in spite of herself.

"Not for much longer. Stop dawdling!" the man growled, pulling her after him.

"There's no need to hang on to me," Selby protested. "I'm perfectly all right."

"Whatever you say." He let go of her arm, and her feet, encountering a patch of wet seaweed, flew out from under her.

"You'll drown before the tide covers the rocks at this rate," he said, hauling her unceremoniously to her feet.

"I have no intention of drowning!" snapped Selby. "I'll have you know I'm a very strong swimmer."

His grip on her arm did not slacken, no matter how much she wriggled. *"I'm* equipped to swim for it, but you're not. I warn you, that water's colder than the hubs of hell."

"The hubs of hell are *hot!"* she protested, unpleasantly conscious of the water creeping around her feet now, staining her new tan leather boots.

"You know, you're the sort of woman who deserves to be left on a rock in the middle of the Atlantic," her rescuer said. "Not an ounce of gratitude in your entire body."

"It so happens I was about to leave when you rose up like the black hulk of the sea," she said haughtily.

"Like hell you were! You were mooning at the water like a hypnotized newt," he said. "You were attached to that rock like a bloody barnacle. Watch it!" He took a firmer grip on her arm.

"How much farther?" she gasped. This was not the way she'd come down to the water's edge, and she realized with a shudder that the path she'd taken was already underwater.

"We just have to negotiate this rock pool and we're there," he assured her, splashing nonchalantly through the water, which seemed to be swirling around them now in a most unnerving manner.

The pool was quite shallow, but to Selby it seemed filled with particularly slippery weeds. Twice she stumbled and fell to her knees, soaking her boots and jeans before he hauled her upright again. He'd been right about the water; it was so cold it felt like an amputation.

Finally the rocks stopped sliding out from under her and they were on dry ground. "Oh!" said Selby, breathing hard. "Oh, Lord!"

"Consider yourself lucky," said her deliverer, letting go of her arm. "A few more minutes and you would have been food for the fish."

"I doubt that," she said disdainfully, then caught his eye and muttered, "But thank you anyway."

She looked at him properly for the first time. He really did resemble some kind of watery demon, done up in that wet suit. His eyes were not dark green as she'd first thought, but black. Black as pitch under heavy brows. Not a nice-looking face at all. Much too craggy.

"This person you're waiting for?" he asked. "Will he—or she—know where to find you?"

"It's a he," Selby replied, "and he won't, because he doesn't know me."

"Doesn't that rather complicate things?"

"I mean we've never met," she explained. "He doesn't know me from a hole in the ground." But he was going to. Oh, yes, he was going to!

"And you were sitting out there on Suicide Rocks waiting for a total stranger to turn up out of the blue!" He shook his head. "You are one strange lady."

She tilted her chin combatively. "Not strange at all. He lives in the lighthouse. I was just waiting for him to come back."

His brows rose a millimeter. "That's where Danny Forest lives."

She nodded. "I know. It's Mr. Forest I'm waiting for." She wished this man would go away. Her feet felt cold, and she wanted to get dry shoes from the car. "Well, thanks again," she said, starting to squelch away.

"What do you want with Danny Forest?" he called after her.

"I really don't think," she called frostily over her shoulder, "that it's any of your business."

"That's where you're wrong," he said. "It's very much my business, since I'm the guy you're looking for."

She stopped in midstride. "What?"

"I'm Danny Forest." He smiled. He had uneven, but remarkably white teeth.

Selby stood, dismayed. "You can't be Danny Forest," she said. "It's impossible."

"Do you think we could continue this conversation indoors?" he suggested. "I'm liable to get pneumonia if I don't get into some warm clothes."

"But you *can't* be!" insisted Selby. "You're much too young."

"I'm older than I look. It comes of leading a virtuous life."

Her voice rose an octave. "It's not possible, I tell you."

"Try telling that to my parents," he said. "Now look, be reasonable. Come inside and we can discuss who I am over a cup of hot coffee."

He hitched the mesh bag over his shoulder and led the way up the path. Selby followed, noting his pantherlike lope, the taut leanness of his buttocks. He might not look like a film star, but he moved like an athlete.

He opened the door of the lighthouse, and the blond Labrador, barking its head off with excitement, danced around them.

"Shut up, Barkis!" he yelled. "Don't be afraid of Barkis," he said to Selby. "She makes a hell of a racket, but she wouldn't hurt a fly."

"Well-named dog," Selby murmured over the clamor, and Barkis, encouraged by this approval, barked louder than ever.

"Out," said Danny, pushing the dog out the front door. "Out, girl!" He slammed the door behind her and the sound of barking diminished.

"She'll stop in a minute," he said. "She's always vocal when she's been shut up. It's her way of registering protest."

"It certainly seems to be effective," Selby observed. "They must be able to hear her in St. John's."

Danny grinned, then said, "Just a sec," and went to empty the contents of his mesh bag into a plastic bucket.

The ground floor of the lighthouse was fitted out like a laboratory. Counters had been built into the circular walls, and these held an assortment of trays containing what looked to Selby's untrained eye like a variety of rubbish from the beach. There were also several microscopes, a laptop computer and a steel filing cabinet. A quantity of rocks and sea-urchin shells lay on a trestle table, along with the mounted skeleton of some sort of bird.

"This way," said Danny, indicating an iron ladder painted bright red.

She started to climb. "I call this Jacob's Ladder," he said, coming up after her. "Hard on the legs, but heaven when you get there."

The second floor was the kitchen/dining area, with a sturdy table, two ladder-back chairs and a small stove for cooking. There was also a propane stove for heat and he knelt to light it.

"I don't know about you, but I'm cold," he said.

She squinted down at her sodden boots and legs. "So am I!"

He immediately became businesslike. "Take your boots off—and your jeans. I'll dry them on the stove."

"Certainly not." She inched toward the ladder. "I have dry things in the case in my car—"

"Wrap this around you." He pulled a tablecloth from one of the shelves. "Your jeans won't take long to dry."

She rejected the tablecloth, but removed her boots, saying firmly, "My jeans aren't that wet. I prefer to keep them on."

"Suit yourself." He straightened, and she noticed again the grace of his movements. "You'll find a kettle by the sink, so make yourself useful and put it on while I go up and dress."

She set her lips firmly. "I don't want any coffee, thank you."

"I do, sweetie, and since I make the best coffee in Newfoundland, you'd be wise to accept a cup."

"I don't want any..." she began again, but he was gone.

She had a mind to pull on her sodden boots and leave, but perhaps a cup of hot coffee wasn't such a bad idea, after all. She *was* cold....

She went to the sink, filled the kettle and put it on the stove. Then she looked around. Downstairs had been utilitarian, but this room was delightfully cozy. The wooden floor had been painted a cheerful shade of yellow and strewn with blue, red and yellow braided rugs. Two blue rattan chairs with yellow and blue

cushions were drawn up to the stove. Cupboards and
a fridge had been skillfully set into the circular walls.
There seemed to be more windows than was usual in a
lighthouse, and she went to one of them and looked
out. There was nothing to see except fog, pressing
against the glass like cotton wool. It was as if the
lighthouse were the only solid thing in the universe,
and everything else was fluid, intangible. All she could
hear was the murmur of the sea breaking on the rocks
below. Even the gulls were silent.

She gave a little shiver and turned back into the
room, moving closer to the stove for comfort, and after a while her jeans started to steam.

Danny came down the red-painted ladder from the
third level as silently as a cat. He seemed taller than
ever in a black turtleneck sweater and gray cords, and
now she could see that his hair was jet black like his
eyes and shiny as a raven's wing. He had the same sort
of cragginess as a young Abraham Lincoln—not the
kind of looks she'd ever admired, but not as unattractive as she'd first thought.

"Cold?" he asked, seeing her huddled by the stove.
He took a jar of coffee beans out of the fridge and put
a couple of spoonfuls into a coffee grinder. "This will
warm you up."

Not really wanting to use the bathroom, but curi-
ous to see some more of the lighthouse, she asked
where it was, and he directed her upstairs. "One floor
up from the living room. The small door at the far end
of my bedroom."

She thanked him and climbed the iron ladder, stopping briefly to look at the living room. More blue and

yellow, but with bold touches of apple green in the cotton slipcovers on the two chairs. Again shelves had been built into the curve of the wall, holding books this time, a small television and VCR, a tape deck and a radio.

His bedroom was austere. A large iron bedstead painted yellow, and covered with a white spread. A yellow kitchen chair served as bedside table and was laden with books. There was also a curtained-off corner that Selby decided was where he kept his clothes. The little bathroom consisted of a shower stall, a minute washbasin, toilet and a small mirrored wall cabinet.

She washed her hands—the water was surprisingly hot—and looked into the cabinet mirror. The damp had tousled her hair into a riot of curling tendrils, and her delicate skin glowed with health. Newfoundland seemed to agree with her, she thought. She hadn't looked this good in weeks.

The aroma of freshly brewed coffee greeted her when she returned to the kitchen. "You're in luck," Danny said. "Lori baked blueberry muffins this morning. She makes the best blueberry muffins you've ever tasted." A tray holding a coffeepot, jug of cream and mugs sat on the stool. "Find a place for these, will you?" he said, handing Selby a plate with two muffins on it.

Not entirely thrilled at being ordered around, she put the plate on the floor beneath the stool. "Now, have a seat," he told her. "Do you take sugar?"

"No."

"Good! I don't, either, and I don't think I have any."

This was becoming altogether too social, and she said firmly, "Now look, Mr. Forest—"

"Danny." He passed her a mug of steaming coffee. "Help yourself to cream. I heated the muffins. Let's eat them while they're still warm."

"I've already eaten two at the store."

"Have another one, then."

"Never mind the muffins!" snapped Selby, "We have business to discuss."

He grinned and took a muffin. "Scuba diving always makes me ravenous. I can't discuss anything until I've had something to eat. Besides, I don't even know your name."

"It's Selby Maitland—"

"Pretty name. It suits you."

"—and I've flown over from England because I'm looking for—"

"—Danny Forest. And now you've found him."

"I *haven't*," she said severely. "You're far too young to be the Danny Forest I want."

"I'd have thought I was just the right age," he said through a mouthful of muffin.

She frowned. "The Daniel Forest I'm looking for was a soldier in 1942."

"Ah, well! I've never been a soldier."

"And you weren't even born in 1942." He was beginning to get seriously on her nerves.

"I wasn't even a gleam in my father's eye. I was born in 1964." She did some quick mental arithmetic.

Just four years older than she was and definitely *not* the man she'd come all this way to see.

She looked at him suspiciously. "Is your father named Daniel?"

"No. And he was born in 1940, so it isn't him, either. Look, are you going to eat that muffin or not?"

"Oh, you have it, for heaven's sake!" She thrust the plate at him. A thought struck her. "Do you have a grandfather?"

He took a big bite of muffin before saying, "Doesn't everybody?"

"I mean *here*," she said impatiently.

"Not here. No." Did she imagine it, or was he being evasive? "Why are you so anxious to find him?"

Selby became uncharacteristically cautious. Normally she would have blurted out the reason without a moment's thought, but she didn't really trust this man. Suppose his grandfather *was* the Daniel Forest she was looking for, and he discovered why she was so desperate to find him? It was unlikely he'd volunteer information that would get a close relative in trouble.

"It seems he knew my grandmother during the war," she said with elaborate nonchalance. "I thought it would be fun to look him up. I . . . I promised Gran I would." In spite of herself, her voice grew husky.

He brushed crumbs off his fingers. He had nice hands, long fingered and strong. "You came all this way just to look up an old friend of your grandmother's?"

"Not entirely. I'm a journalist. The magazine I work for sent me over to get some stories about Canadian life." Not strictly true, but plausible.

"What sort of stories?" He was leaning back in his chair, surveying her speculatively, and she found herself noticing what long eyelashes he had. Long and thick and sooty black.

"Oh, human interest." She took a sip of coffee. "Feminism in small-town Canada, that sort of thing."

"And have you found a story in Savage Harbour?" he asked, getting up and going to the window.

"Well, I don't know yet. I've only just arrived."

"And not about to leave for a while."

"What?" She joined him. The fog had turned from cotton wool to dense gray metal.

"It's what's referred to around here as a regular ripsnorter," Danny informed her. "You can't drive in this."

"I'm British. I'm used to fog," she said. "I'll drive very slowly—"

"And go straight over a cliff," he said. "No way, lady! We're not thrilled about scooping up tourists around here."

"But I need to get back to Halifax," she protested. To start searching from scratch again, because the more she thought about it, the less likely it seemed that Danny's grandfather was her man. If he was, Danny would surely have mentioned it by now. And she only had a couple of weeks left. She *had* to find him!

"So, you'll get back to Halifax a day late. Ripsnorters don't usually last long."

He looked capable of keeping her here by force. "Then I'll have to find a hotel." He picked up the coffeepot and refilled their mugs. "Sorry to disappoint you, but there's no such thing in Savage Harbour."

"Well, I can't stay here!" she said firmly.

He raised his eyebrows in mock horror. "What an improper suggestion. I only have one bed."

Selby had the kind of skin that colors readily, and now she turned a delicate shade of pink. "I wasn't suggesting—"

"Of course you weren't. Relax." He handed her the mug of coffee. "Lori, over at the store, can probably fix you up with a bed for the night."

She was still reluctant. "I don't think it's really necessary."

"It is."

Since she was blessed with a healthy share of it herself, she recognized obstinacy when she ran across it. "Oh, all right!"

Arguing with him would be just a waste of time. All she had to do was walk over to the store, get into her car and drive away. He was hardly likely to come after her. She finished her coffee. "I'd better go to the store, then, and arrange it."

"We'll phone from here," he said, looking at her shrewdly. "We don't want you toppling over Suicide Rocks."

"There's no need to phone," she protested, flushing guiltily. "Really. I've taken up too much of your time as it is."

He smiled. A smile that appeared to Selby decidedly crafty. "I'm on vacation—my time's my own. Besides, Lori's store isn't the most comfortable place to wait for nightfall. You're more than welcome to sit here where it's warm. There are magazines, books...or you can go upstairs and watch a movie on the VCR.''

"All the comforts of home," she said sarcastically.

But sarcasm was clearly wasted on him. He smiled amiably. "Exactly."

When he'd phoned the store and arranged for her to spend the night there, he told her he was going downstairs to do some work.

"I thought you said you were on vacation," she accused him.

"So I am. But I'm an amateur naturalist, and I found some interesting specimens when I was diving. I want to take a look at them."

"What sort of specimens?"

"Oh, some interesting types of seaweed, for one, and there's a large clam worm I want to dissect." He grinned. "Want to watch?"

"No, thanks." She shuddered. "Dissecting worms isn't one of my favorite things, as a matter of fact."

"You must tell me what one of your favorite things is sometime," he drawled. "Perhaps we could do it together."

He looked quite innocent, but Selby detected the note of invitation in his voice. "I'll stay here and do some reading." She picked up a magazine and riffled through the pages. "You go on down to your worm."

When he'd clattered to the bottom level, she threw the magazine aside. She was in no mood for reading. Ever since the discovery that this was the wrong Daniel Forest, she'd been growing progressively restless. If he hadn't bulldozed her into staying, she'd be inching her way back to St. John's by now, and then she could

get off this godforsaken rock and get back to Halifax
as quickly as possible. Once there she could get reor-
ganized, perhaps go to a Canadian detective agency,
and set about finding the proper Daniel Forest. She
only had twelve days left, and she'd promised Maisy.
Well, not promised her in so many words, but it was
something she *had* to do. It was her way of repaying
her grandmother for all those years of devotion.

She prowled around the little circular room like a
caged animal, picking up books, leafing through
magazines. Most of them dealt with nature, but there
were also some novels, some poetry, some political
journals. An eclectic reader, apparently, this Danny
Forest.

If only she had more time, it might have been fun to
get to know him better. But she had no time to spare
for that kind of thing. None. This wasn't a holiday, it
was a vendetta, and she couldn't afford to let herself
forget that.

She threw herself into one of the chairs and tried to
relax the tension in her neck, the way she'd learned in
yoga classes. It didn't seem to work right away, but
after a while the comfortable chair and the warmth
from the stove combined to lull her into a state of
drowsiness. Slowly her eyelids drooped and she fell
into a troubled doze.

That was how Danny found her, her head cradled
on her arm, her lashes casting a shadow on her cheeks.

"Teatime!" he said, pouring water into the kettle
and putting it on the stove.

She jerked awake, instantly alert. The room was nearly dark, the only light the glow of the stove. "How... how long have I been asleep?"

He took a teapot from the cupboard and started to rinse the mugs. "About two hours."

She leapt up and went to one of the windows, tripping over Barkis, who was sprawled on the rug. The fog was like a solid wall. "It's worse than ever," she wailed.

"Mmm, a bit." He topped up the milk jug. "Do you like the milk in first or afterward? Or do you like your tea clear? I don't have any lemon, I'm afraid."

But Selby wasn't interested in tea. "What's it going to be like tomorrow?" she demanded. "Have you heard a weather report? Is it going to clear?"

"Questions, questions! I've no idea." He pressed a switch on one of the brass lamps attached to the wall. The sudden light highlighted the contours of his face, accentuating the strong cheekbones, the deep-set eyes. "The only thing to do in a ripsnorter is sit it out."

"I don't have the time to sit it out," she snarled. "Don't you understand? I don't have time." She ran her hands distractedly through her short curls.

He rinsed out the pot with a little of the hot water before putting two tea bags into it. "What *I* don't understand," he said, "is why it's so important. I mean, he's only a friend of the family, isn't he? You carry on as if he were your link to a fortune."

She came away from the window, her alarm bells clanging. But all she could think of to say was, "I promised Gran. I promised."

"Why didn't she come with you, if it's so important?"

Selby fingered the garnet ring on her finger, the one Maisy had always worn. "She died four months ago."

"I'm sorry." He sounded genuinely sympathetic. "You were close?"

She nodded, and blinked her large gray eyes—eyes that were suddenly bright with tears. "She brought me up."

"Then of course you must find her friend." He poured boiling water into the pot and set it down with the mugs.

"That's easy for you to say, but I've got less than two weeks left," she said, using irritation to mask her distress, "and I don't know how to begin. I can't look up all the D. Forest's in every province in Canada."

"That won't be necessary." He sounded quite casual. "I'm pretty sure the Daniel Forest you're looking for is my grandfather—" he started to pour the tea "—and he'll be back from vacation soon. Milk?"

CHAPTER THREE

SHE STARED AT HIM, outraged. "Your *grandfather*?"

"Yes. Nice guy, you'll like him."

She could have hit him. "Why the hell didn't you mention it before?"

"I had to be careful."

"Careful? *Careful?* Of what?" She realized she was shouting.

"Of you. You said you were a journalist. Scotia Trading isn't wild about publicity."

"And what is Scotia Trading when it's at home?" she asked truculently.

"The family firm. We own extensive harbor facilities in Halifax, among other things."

"So your family's rich. *Very* rich?"

"That's putting it a bit crudely," he said, "but ... yes. However, it's company policy to keep a low profile. Granddad, particularly, hates publicity."

Selby clenched her fists till the nails dug into her palms. The idea of Daniel Forest sitting on all that money while Maisy had spent her life struggling to make ends meet made her blood boil.

"I can assure you I'm not interested in writing about your grandfather *or* his business," she said tightly.

"It's not his business anymore," Danny said. "It's mine. Granddad's retired."

"Whatever!" She pushed irritably at the silky curls that tumbled over her forehead.

"You could always write about me." He passed her a mug of tea. "Life in a lighthouse. How a lonely bachelor pines for something more exciting than clam worms. Something along those lines."

"Why don't you invite someone to share your holiday with you if you're so lonely?" she snapped.

He looked at her face for a minute as if memorizing every detail, then said, "I'm between 'someones' at the moment. How about you?"

"Me?"

"Yes. A pretty woman like you must have a string of males panting to take her to their lonely lighthouses."

"I left them behind in England," she said, pouring milk into her tea. "Besides, I have work to do—"

"And an old friend of your grandmother's to look up." He shot her a glance as piercing as an arrow.

"Well, at least," she said grudgingly, "you've saved me from going on a wild-goose chase."

"I wouldn't have let you do that...once I got to know the sort of person you are." He still looked at her steadily, and she had to make an effort not to glance away from those glittering jet black eyes.

"You think you know what sort of person I am?"

"I believe you're honest," he said. "I don't think you have any ulterior motives."

She sat down again and leaned forward, hoping it would look as if the warmth from the stove had brought the sudden flush to her cheeks. "I'm just interested in getting a little local color for my magazine," she said, "not writing exposés."

He said quietly, "There's nothing to expose."

"I'm sure there isn't." Poor dolt, she thought. He was going to be upset when he learned the truth.

He took a swallow of tea, then asked casually, "When did you say your grandmother met Granddad?"

"In 1942. He *was* in England during the war, wasn't he?" But she knew the answer. Daniel Forest might lie about everything else, but he couldn't lie about his army service.

Danny nodded. "For a short time, before he was sent to the European front."

Long enough to deceive Maisy. "I'm looking forward to meeting your grandfather." *You'd better believe I am!*

"Well, he'll be back in Canada in a week. He's gone with my parents on a tour of the Norwegian fjords."

She'd almost forgotten the European grand tour. "How nice." Remembering how Maisy had had to scrimp and save to take a week's holiday in Cornwall, she found it hard to keep the ice out of her voice.

"Of course Dad had to practically drug Mom to get her away," Danny continued conversationally. "She can't bear to leave her garden, especially in the fall."

"I'm sure the fjords will more than make up for it." His mother sounded thoroughly spoiled to Selby. The sort of overindulged woman she had no time for.

Danny leaned down to scratch Barkis between the ears before saying, "What's bothering you, Selby?"

Oh, Lord, did it show that she was seething with indignation? Was she so transparent? "Nothing." She looked at her wristwatch. "I think I'd better be going over to the store. They'll be wondering what's happened to me."

"They won't. They know you're with me."

She tried again, loudly. "I'd like to go to the store, please."

"Okay, okay!" He rose to his feet. "If that's what you want..."

"It is." But she didn't object when he came with her. She would have had difficulty keeping to the path in the fog. Even with the powerful flashlight Danny carried she could barely see her feet.

But man and dog were as surefooted as mountain goats, and Selby clung to Danny's arm, glad he was there to guide her, even if he did come from an unfortunate family.

"Thank you for tea," she said when they were outside the store, "and for drying my boots."

He bowed in mock formality and handed her the suitcase they'd retrieved from her car. "You're more than welcome. I shall, as they say, see you around." Giving her a brief smile, he strode off into the thick mantle of fog, Barkis at his heels.

There were several people in the store, some drinking coffee, others just leaning against the counter chatting, and they all looked up when Selby came in.

"Hi, Selby!" said Lori. "Come to check in?"

"If I may." She closed the door behind her and came into the room, slightly disconcerted by the quiet that had fallen and the unabashed curiosity of the other customers.

"This is Selby. She's waitin' out the fog in Savage Harbour," Lori informed them.

"Sure is a regular ripsnorter," said a weathered old man seated near the potbellied stove, which seemed to be the focal point of the store.

"Do you think it'll last long?" asked Selby, although now that she knew Daniel Forest wouldn't be in the country for another week, it didn't really matter.

The old man shrugged. "Coupla days, mebbe less, hard to tell."

A heavyset woman wrapped in a man's oilskin coat regarded Selby suspiciously. "From away? Don't recognize the accent."

"She's from England. Here on a visit," said Lori, who seemed to have appointed herself Selby's representative.

"I ain't never been to England," the woman said.

"You ain't hardly been to St. John's, Clara," Lori pointed out. "Now stop starin' at the poor girl like she was swept up on the beach or somethin'." She smiled at Selby. "Want me to show you your room?"

Selby nodded. "Please."

"C'mon, then."

The room Selby was to sleep in was at the top of a steep staircase. "It's our daughter Shari's room," Lori explained, adding with a certain pride, "She's at the university, studyin' to be a nurse."

It was tiny, but clean and cheerful, with posters of rock stars pinned to the wall, and a Raggedy Ann doll on the bed. "Bathroom's down the hall," Lori said, "but the water ain't hot yet on account of the boiler bein' off most of the day." She turned at the door on her way out. "I can fix you some crab cakes for your supper, otherwise it'll have to be hamburgers."

"Crab cakes, please," said Selby.

The older woman nodded approvingly. "Good choice."

Left alone, Selby looked around for a place to put the photograph of Maisy she had brought with her. There was no table or chair on which to set the leather fold-up frame, so she took her nightshirt and sponge bag out of her case, and then stood the case on end to use as a stand for Maisy's picture. Having her grandmother's picture beside her made her feel less lonely. She and Maisy would have had a good laugh about the day's adventures. Her grandmother had always managed to find something to laugh about—except back in 1942, which Selby now intended to do something about, even if it was too late to be of any practical use to Maisy.

"It's the principle of the thing, darling," she muttered at the picture, because she wasn't *absolutely* sure her grandmother would have approved of her plan.

When she went downstairs for her supper, there were two new arrivals. Lori introduced them. "This here's my husband, Mac." A bald mountain of a man smiled at Selby. "And this is our youngest daughter, Beverly."

Beverly was a pretty, but sulky-looking girl of about fifteen. She gave Selby a brief uninterested glance before returning to the fascinating business of examining her freshly painted nails.

"Lori tells me you come from England," Mac boomed. "Now there's a country I'd like to see."

"I'd rather go to Los Angeles," declared Beverly, holding out her hand to get the full effect of her manicure. "There's more goin' on there. We learned about England in the fifth grade. Sounded real boring."

"Everythin's boring to you, Bev," her mother remarked placidly, "including your homework. Do you have much tonight?"

Beverly tossed her long blond hair. "I did most of it in the bus, 'cept the biology. I'm savin' the biology for Danny."

"You mustn't take advantage of Danny, Bev," her father said. "He may not want to help you with your homework tonight. He most likely wants to spend the time with his lady friend from England." He gestured at Selby.

"He *always* helps me with my homework," replied Beverly, glaring at Selby. "I'll fail the exam if I don't get help. Then you'll be sorry."

"That'll do, Bev!" her mother said sharply. "An' stop wavin' your hands about like that. Makes you look touched." She turned to Selby. "Do you want fries or mashed with your cakes? Fries is easiest."

"Fries, please," said Selby, getting the hint.

"Good choice," approved Lori, turning her attention to the stove.

While she waited for her meal, Selby sipped a soft drink and fielded the questions the customers threw at her. They wanted to know about the state of commercial fishing off the English coast, the rate of unemployment, and if Selby had ever seen the Queen. Questions to which she felt sure she gave disappointing answers.

"Ain't much fishing goin' on these days, though, thanks to them government quotas," one gnarled man said.

Lori nodded. "And if things weren't hard enough already, two of our fishing boats went down a coupla years back—lost every man. Terrible. Tragic." She turned the crab cakes over in the pan with a sizzle, then nodded toward a woman huddled by the stove. "She lost her husband an' her son," she said softly. "She ain't got no one now."

"But she still stays here?" Selby said.

"Where's she gonna go? Her friends is here." Lori dished up the cakes, added a generous scoop of french-fried potatoes and said, "Eat up before it gets cold."

Selby didn't need coaxing. She was hungry, and the cakes were delicious, the chips crisp and golden. The scrunchions, however, she left untasted, still suspicious of these cubes of fried pork fat that seemed to be served with everything in Newfoundland.

While she ate, she planned out an article about Savage Harbour, having decided that she might as well stay where she was and get something out of it, rather than go back to Halifax to wait for the Forest family. She had just swallowed the last piece of crab cake when Danny arrived. She had the distinct impression the lights grew brighter, as if his arrival had brought a surge of extra power into the room.

"You're late!" Beverly accused him. "I thought you wasn't coming."

"And miss your mother's crab cakes?" He hung his foul-weather jacket on a peg by the door. "You should know better than that. And it's 'were not coming,' not 'wasn't,' cupcake."

"Were not coming," the girl said, smiling at him. Selby noticed how pretty she was when she wiped the sullen expression off her face.

"I trust you've left some for me," he said to Selby, perching his athletic frame on the stool beside her. His thick hair gleamed, dark as a raven's wing, and his smile crinkled the corners of his eyes. Selby didn't know why she should be so pleased to see him, but she was. Ridiculously pleased.

While Lori cooked his supper, Danny helped Beverly with her biology homework. She had installed herself on the stool on his other side, and she kept touching his sleeve and smiling up into his face, pretending to pore over her books so that her long blond hair brushed his hand.

The girl had a giant-size crush on him, Selby thought, remembering her own teenage years and the hopeless love she'd felt for the local vet, a happily married man of thirty-five with a string of children. At the time she had thought she might die of longing. Her grandmother had been the only person she'd dared to confide in, for she'd known Maisy wouldn't belittle her hopeless passion. Maisy had known that one was never too young to suffer.

Danny closed the textbook, saying, "So you could say that the barnacle welds its head to a rock and spends its life kicking food into its mouth with its feet."

Beverly pulled a face. "Gross!"

He grinned at her. "Not gross at all. It's very practical. Mind you, I don't recommend it for humans. Your mother would spend her life cleaning the floor." He put the book into her hands. "Now, go and write your essay before you forget everything I've been saying."

The girl pleaded, "Come and help me write it?"

"No way, cupcake. That's not part of our agreement. I want to talk to Selby now."

Beverly's expression reverted to sulky resentment. "It'll be your fault if I fail my test."

"I'll try and live with that knowledge." He turned to Selby. "You are going to stay in Savage Harbour for a bit, aren't you? When the fog lifts there's plenty to see, believe me."

"If it ever does." She finished the last chip and pushed her plate away. "I'm beginning to think Newfoundland's got the edge on England when it comes to fog."

"Please stay, Selby. It would be so...so pleasant."

He sounded utterly sincere, and her heart gave a funny little flutter. "Well...I could write that article."

Beverly asked loudly, "How long you two known each other, then?"

Selby looked at her watch. "About seven hours."

"Not nearly long enough," Danny said. "It's irresponsible for a woman like you to blow into my life for only seven hours. Probably illegal, as well." He smiled, a disarming smile that caused her heart to flutter again. "It's not fair on a guy."

"Here you are." Lori put a heaping plate of crab cakes in front of him. "Now, Bev, go on in the back and do your homework, like Danny told you."

Beverly scooped up her books, her blue eyes burning with resentment. "I'm sick of everybody ordering me around like some dumb kid."

"Then stop behavin' like one," suggested her mother.

Beverly muttered something fortunately incomprehensible and went out, slamming the door behind her.

"Girls!" remarked Mac, who had sauntered behind the counter to help himself to a cup of coffee. "I never could figger 'em out."

"You could never figger out anythin' that didn't have fins an' scales on it," said his wife fondly. She addressed the two at the counter. "There's gingerbread or ice cream for dessert."

"If the weather clears tomorrow I plan to take the dory out," Danny said after they'd demolished their gingerbread. "Will you come along?" He imitated a tour guide. "The coastline around here is magnificent, with many hidden coves and villages. The wildlife is spectacular. I can promise you puffins and sea gulls, possibly seals."

She laughed, wondering how she could ever have thought he was unattractive. He was really almost handsome when you got to know him. "What about blue-footed boobies?"

"I'm afraid boobies don't frequent these waters, ma'am," he said, continuing the game.

"That's too bad. I've always longed to see a blue-footed booby."

He returned to his normal voice. "The only booby will be yours truly in waders. Will you come?"

"And what if the fog doesn't lift?"

"We could spend the day—" he raised his eyebrows suggestively "—indoors."

"Sounds most unhealthy to me," she said lightly.

"We could play Scrabble," he said innocently. "You're looking at a champion."

"And you're looking at a journalist," she warned him. "Words are my game, remember?"

"We could always settle for another kind of game." Those dark wicked eyes of his gleamed with innuendo.

"We could, but we're not going to," she said firmly.

"Then I'd better pray for good weather," he said, "because at this rate you could break my heart."

"I refuse to believe your heart's as fragile as that," she said, smiling, but she was faintly puzzled at her reaction. She didn't usually have this wild urge to say, "Yes, please!" when a man chatted her up.

A newcomer came into the store and spotted Danny. "Seen two dovekies over at Fletcher's Cove today, Danny," he said, coming over to him. "Thought you'd wanna know."

"But they don't come in to shore this time of year," Danny protested. "Are you sure they were dovekies, Wilf?"

"Sure I'm sure," Wilf declared. "I seen them plain."

"You haven't been into the screech, have you?" Danny asked.

"I'm a teetotaler these days, Danny, an' you know it." Wilf grinned.

"That does it!" said Danny to Selby. "The Scrabble will have to wait. Fog or not, we'll take the dory over to Fletcher's Cove first thing tomorrow morning."

The mention of dovekies, whatever they were, seemed to have driven all thoughts of flirtation out of his head, and Selby felt mildly put out. His assumption that she'd follow his command like a well-trained dog rankled, too.

Smiling sweetly, she said, "I have other things to do in the morning." He looked at her, surprised. "Like what?"

"I'm staying on to write an article, remember?"

He waved this aside. "Sure I do. Write about the dovekies."

"I don't think our readers would be desperately interested," she said, "even if they knew what they were."

The corner of his mouth twitched. "Do you know?"

She shook her curly head. "I haven't the faintest."

"I can see I've got my work cut out repairing the gaps in your education," he said with mock severity. "Dovekies, my girl, are small black-and-white pelagic birds with short tails. They only come ashore to breed and are rarely sighted. Frankly, I think Wilf's hallucinating, but we can't afford to ignore him."

"*You* can't," she said. "I'm not interested."

"Nonsense! An embryonic naturalist like you?"

She giggled. "Who says I'm an embryonic naturalist?"

"It's obvious. Only naturalists sit around on wet rocks gazing at a foggy sea. I should know. I do it all the time."

"I wasn't gazing at the sea. I was eating my lunch."

"You were gazing at the sea, sweetheart. The first thing I saw when I surfaced were those beautiful eyes of yours. You were riveted."

"Well..." She hesitated. "I thought you were a walrus."

His brows shot up. "A walrus!"

"Yes. I've always wanted to see one."

"Sorry to disappoint you."

"Oh, well—" she gave a comic sigh "—maybe you could grow a mustache?"

"I did once. I looked like a B-movie villain."

"They complained, did they?" she said. "The 'someones'?"

He looked at her, uncomprehending at first, then he smiled. "All the 'someones' have become 'no ones' since I met you," he said softly.

The universe Selby inhabited seemed to rock very slightly. He was the sexiest man she'd ever encountered, and the kind of verbal play they'd just engaged in was playing with fire.

"Honestly," she said, "I'm not sure I'm coming. You'd better not count on me."

To her relief he appeared not to have heard. "I'll be here at six o'clock!" He swung his lean body off the stool and pulled a handful of bills out of his pocket.

"In the morning?" she asked faintly.

"Dovekies don't sleep in, sweetheart." He snapped his fingers for Barkis, who was dozing by the stove. "And wear a warm jacket. It's cold on the water." There he was, ordering her around again.

"I'm not sure I'm coming," she reminded him.

But he merely smiled and leaned down to drop an unexpected kiss on the corner of her mouth. "See you!"

His lips had barely grazed her, but the touch of his mouth was like fire.

"More coffee?" Lori was holding the pot over her cup.

"No, thank you. I won't sleep if I have any more caffeine." Although she was so tired a gallon of coffee wouldn't have kept her awake. "I think I'll head for bed."

She needed an early night if she was meeting Danny at six. Of course she was going to meet him—wild horses wouldn't have kept her away.

Her room faced the sea, and she could hear it whispering and murmuring on the rocks. If it had been a clear night, she would have been able to see the lighthouse, although, gazing out the little window, she imagined she could make out its muted shape. Would Danny go straight up that red ladder to his aerie? Or would he check on something in the laboratory first?

She pulled the curtains across the window with an irritated twitch. If he wanted to jump off Suicide Rocks and swim the Atlantic, it was no concern of hers. She must remember he was simply the man who was her contact with Maisy's Danny. Nothing more.

The feeling of electricity between them, the erotic tension, was nothing more than passing lust and should be recognized as such.

In the bathroom she discovered she'd left her toothpaste behind at the last motel. Well, there were several good things to be said for staying in the village's general store. Being able to purchase toothpaste after closing time was one of them.

She hadn't undressed yet, so she made her way downstairs, hoping someone from the family was still up. She'd heard the last of the customers leaving when she'd been trying to see the lighthouse.

The back room was empty. Beverly's books were neatly stacked on the table, her half-written essay lying, with the pen still uncapped, beside it. The main light was off. Selby could hear Mac and Lori chatting together in the store.

She started to open the door when she heard Lori say, "Danny's like his grandfather. Old Daniel would have behaved just the same." She ran the tap and Mac's reply was lost.

"Anyway," she went on, "I think it's a good thing she kept the baby. She needs somethin' to love in her life. Is Danny goin' on payin' after she gets a job, d'you know?"

"Figgers he don't have to, I guess," Mac said.

He was close to the door, and Selby jumped guiltily; but she couldn't stop listening, even though every word was like a splash of cold water. She had to hear more.

"You know what Danny's like about that kinda thing," Mac said. "It's more'n your life's worth to ask personal questions. He just likes to forget he had any hand in it."

"Poor little cow," said Lori. "Must be lonely for her in Toronto…not knowin' anyone. Must be hard."

"Yeah, but Danny thought it best she went away," Mac said, "an' after all, it's more his affair than ours. We got no right to interfere."

Selby didn't wait to hear any more. She turned and crept as quietly as she could up the cold and unforgiving stairs.

CHAPTER FOUR

SHE WAS TIRED, but she couldn't sleep. She lay rigid in the narrow bed, her mind racing.

What was that old saying? The apple never falls far from the tree! Well, this apple had not only fallen, it was rotten to the core.

"Danny's like his grandfather," Lori had said. Selby could still hear the words, still feel the shock of them, because it was clear now Danny had *also* fathered a child and then, even though it sounded as if he'd shelled out some cash, he'd sent the woman packing. "Poor little cow," Lori had called her, and Mac had grunted in sympathy.

"Just like Gran," Selby muttered, hot, angry tears scalding her cheeks.

Maisy had been an open, warmhearted woman, but during Selby's childhood the subject of her past had always been glossed over. Selby knew her grandfather had been a Canadian soldier posted in Britain during the war, but whenever she had questioned her grandmother about him, Maisy had clammed up. Selby was a perceptive child. She had sensed that the subject was taboo and stopped bothering her grandmother. It was enough that she knew his name had been Danny Forest, and that if she mentioned him, her grandmother's natural cheerfulness ebbed. Selby assumed that he'd died in the war and that his memory was too painful for Maisy to talk about.

Too painful for her even to use his surname. "I don't want to be reminded of him," had been Maisy's explanation.

However, when Maisy was dying, she started talking, a flood of memories that had been suppressed were released, and at last Selby learned the truth.

It was a common-enough story. Maisy had been twenty-three and working in a factory when she'd met Danny Forest at a dance. It had been a case of love at first sight, and the affair progressed rapidly. The war was on, and God alone knew what the outcome would be. The two young people were swept away by their passion.

When Maisy discovered she was pregnant, Danny told her not to worry—he'd marry her on his next leave. Then he was shipped to France, and Maisy never heard from him again. Brokenhearted, she assumed he'd been killed in action.

She was alone in the world, apart from an older sister who refused to have anything more to do with her when she discovered that Maisy had every intention of keeping the child. The child she carried was Maisy's only reason for living. She would rather have died than relinquish it.

She gave birth to a daughter, whom she named Danielle after her dead lover, and then, burying her grief, she proceeded to make a life for herself and her child.

After the war she traced her lover's family, thinking they might want to know about Danielle. It was then she discovered that she'd been betrayed.

Danny Forest was alive and well, and back in Canada. He had been married two years before he went overseas; his promises had all been lies.

A fiercely proud woman, Maisy never tried to contact him again. Not for help, not for money, even though she knew she was entitled to it. She was a dressmaker and managed to make a modest living. "Besides, I had Danielle," she whispered, her eyes filled with pain. "I didn't need his bloody money."

But in her delirium, shortly before her death, she had called for him. Had called him her only love. Had asked over and over again why he'd done it. Why he'd lied. "Oh Danny, Danny!" she'd wept. "Come back. Please come back."

And Selby had stroked her poor thin hands and vowed to make him pay for the years of anguish he had caused.

And now the pattern was being repeated by his grandson. She had a sudden vision of Beverly leaning so eagerly over Danny's shoulder, her eyes filled with trust. If he'd deceived one young woman, there was nothing to stop him from doing the same again. Selby had to do something. She had to.... But what? He was rich. He could buy people off. Send them away. Forget about them. That's what he'd done with the woman Mac and Lori had been talking about. He'd sent her away to Toronto the minute she'd become a problem. Out of sight and out of mind. The bastard!

She turned restlessly and closed her eyes, willing herself to relax, but it was no good. The image of Danny seemed etched on her eyelids, full, sensual mouth smiling, dark eyes filled with promise. "I know what you're up to, mate," she said aloud, opening her eyes again and staring at the glimmering window. "But this time I'm throwing a spanner in your works. I'm on to you, and I'm dammed if I'm going to let you mess up any more lives."

SHE STAGGERED downstairs at six-fifteen the next morning to find Danny sitting at the counter eating bacon and eggs. He waved his fork in greeting. "There's a breeze coming up," he said. "With luck the fog should clear by noon."

She nodded sourly. She needed coffee to rouse her wits, because she knew now, as sure as she was alive, that this man with his lethal charm was as dangerous as Lucifer.

"Be sure to eat a good breakfast," he said. "We won't be stopping for lunch till late."

She replied curtly. "I don't eat breakfast."

"You must this morning. Then if you get seasick, you'll have something to throw up."

"If there's one thing I can't stand," she said, "it's a bossy lecher."

Danny's eyebrows rose perceptibly, but he only said, "Clearly, you're not a morning person."

It was the ideal moment to tell him she wasn't going with him, but just then Beverly came, lips parted, a bit too much lipstick on. "G'morning Danny," she breathed. Selby might have been invisible for all the notice she took of her.

He smiled. That warm, lazy smile that had charmed Selby yesterday but today merely put her on her guard. "How about putting some more bread in the toaster, cupcake?" he said. "And then you'd better be thinking about getting ready for school, hadn't you? I can't drive you today if you miss the bus."

Selby glared at him. What a smooth operator! What a weasel! Driving the girl to school, playing the kind uncle. The kid didn't stand a chance.

Beverly turned a radiant face toward him. "There isn't any school today. It's a study day. I thought mebbe I could go collectin' with you." She waited eagerly for his reply.

"Not today, cupcake," said Danny. "Selby and I are going looking for dovekies."

So, Selby thought, *I'm trapped. If I refuse to go he might take Beverly, instead, and God knows what mischief he might get up to.* "Do you think I might have some coffee, Beverly?" she said.

Beverly, who was looking as stricken as if her entire family had been wiped out by plague, slopped some coffee into a mug and banged it down on the counter. "What do you wanna eat?" she mumbled. "There's oatmeal, eggs with bacon, ham or sausage."

"Just coffee, thank you," Selby said firmly.

"Oatmeal, and bacon and eggs," ordered Danny. "And an order of toast.'

Selby turned on him, wide gray eyes flashing. "I *loathe* oatmeal. I absolutely loathe it." *And I loathe you, too, you misbegotten satyr.*

He held up both hands as if to defend himself. "Okay, okay! You don't need to have oatmeal. But you must have more than coffee."

They finally agreed on an order of toast, which Selby made a great show of nibbling delicately before pushing most of it away.

Danny wrapped what was left in a clean napkin and put it in the small pack beside him. "Believe me, you'll be glad of it when you feel like upchucking later on," he said.

"Is that all you can think about?" she asked waspishly. "Being seasick?"

He smiled. "I just don't want my boat messed up. Remember to lean over the leeward side."

She glared at him. "I've never been seasick in my life."

"You've never been in a dory in your life, either, I bet," he countered.

Beverly, who had witnessed this little scene with great interest, remarked casually, "I never get seasick, do I, Danny? Remember the time we got caught in that squall off Bissel's Head?"

Oh, Lord! thought Selby. *He's already had her out alone in that boat of his, the swine.*

"I'll never forget it, cupcake," said Danny. "I thought your father was going to die on us."

Beverly giggled. "Yeah! An' he's a fisherman," she told Selby. "But it don't seem to make no difference—he still gets seasick all the time."

Danny got up from the stool and went over to the door where Barkis was lying. "Your mom said she could stay here till we get back, Bev," he said. "If you're feeling energetic, you might want to take her for a walk."

Beverly looked at him wistfully. "You sure I can't come with you?"

"Quite sure." He was firm. "Go and visit some of your friends if you can't think of anything else to do."

"They're all such *babies,*" the girl said contemptuously.

"Then think of it as baby-sitting, cupcake, and don't sulk. There's a good girl." She gave him a weak smile. "That's better. See you later."

The dory had an outboard motor, and they soon left the rocks that enclosed Savage Harbour behind. The sea was like oil, but there was a swell, and Selby had to hold on to the sides of the boat to keep her balance.

"Fog's thinning," Danny observed. "Be nice later."

He seemed in his element, an old yachting cap jammed on his thick black hair, rubber hip waders covering his lean flanks. He looked excessively attractive, which contrived to put Selby in an even worse humor. She shivered and pulled the zipper of her jacket higher.

Always discerning, Danny said, "I brought an extra sweater if you're cold. It's in the pack."

"I'm fine—" she set her lips firmly "—thank you." She had a pretty mouth, well molded and sensitive, but this morning it looked as hard as iron.

"I'm not sure I'd agree," he said. "Something seems to be bugging you."

"I'm fine." She stared earnestly into the mist. It might be thinning, but all she could make out was the shadowy bank of cliffs on one side and the endless expanse of sea on the other.

"Not feeling sick, are you?"

"*No!*"

"All right, all right! No need to bite my head off."

"You have a bloody obsession," she snapped.

"And you have a terrible temper," he snapped back.

Conversation languished after this. There was no sound except the *putt-putt* of the outboard and the slap of waves. The water was like dark green satin with occasional strands of kelp drifting on the surface. A moist veil of cold mist pressed against her face, and she could taste salt on her lips.

After a while Danny cut the motor; silence descended like a curtain. He brought out field glasses and scanned the empty ocean, leaning his elbows on his knees to steady himself, patiently searching this way and that.

They drifted for what seemed like hours. She could no longer see the ghostly bank of cliffs. The world was reduced to nothing but water and cloud, forsaken and threatening.

She felt a clutch of dread. It was scary drifting in this cockleshell of a boat, reeling uncomfortably on the empty sea. If he felt so inclined, Danny could pitch her overboard, and no one would be any the wiser.

Screaming in this void would be useless. Even the gulls seemed to have disappeared.

"What exactly are we doing?" she asked, her voice thin in the salty void.

"Shh!"

"I can't see any land. How far are we from land?" Her panic was increasing. "We could drift for miles...."

"Well, if there *were* any dovekies around, you've managed to scare them off," he said, dropping the field glasses.

She took a deep, calming breath. "I'm not used to the sea, I'm a city girl. I don't even know what a dovekie looks like."

"And you're not likely to find out if you keep shouting your fool head off."

"To be honest," she said, glaring, "I don't really give a damn."

He pulled the starter cord and the engine coughed into life. "Why agree to come, then? You knew we'd be going out in the boat."

"Because..." She could hardly tell him she'd appointed herself guardian of Beverly's morals. "Because I... I thought it might be fun."

"It isn't a goddamned disco," he growled, increasing speed.

She didn't bother to answer. She wasn't about to admit she'd been scared—and not just of the limitless sea, but of him. She was beginning to realize she had made another of her impetuous decisions when she agreed to this outing in the first place. For all she knew, he might become violent when she resisted his advances—assuming he made any, of course—and judging from that conversation she'd overheard about babies, and young women being paid off and sent away, advances seemed to be his way of life. Better not have an outright row with him, at least not until they were in sight of land and some people.

A breeze had sprung up and the sea was becoming choppy. Spray stung her cheeks and misted her curls. And then the mist parted and a watery sun gilded the waves and now she could see cliffs, immense and craggy, rising out of a glittering sea that was every shade of green, from milky jade to emerald. As if on cue, birds called and wheeled about them, and a pair of ducks appeared, floating serenely on the cresting waves.

"What are they?" she asked, forgetting for the moment to remain aloof.

"Common eiders." He cut the motor and passed her the glasses.

"They don't look very common to me," she said, focusing. "Do people make eiderdowns from them?"

"You mean comforters?" Selby nodded. "From their down, I guess."

"They're sweet," she said. "I like their funny beaks."

"That's how you identify them." He smiled at her enthusiasm. "It's quite rare to see them this time of year. They usually winter in great rafts off Alaska."

She handed back the glasses. "Do they make up for the dovekies?"

"I think the dovekies were a figment of Wilf's imagination. Either that, or he'd been at the bottle."

He gave her another quick smile. "He's not the most reliable of informants, but it did give me an excuse to get you to myself."

She was instantly on the defensive. "You make it sound as if Savage Harbour were a bustling metropolis. Anyway, why the need for privacy? What exactly did you have in mind?"

She knew the answer to that one, but she wondered if he'd have the gall to be frank about it.

"I want to get to know you better, Selby," he said, "You intrigue me. I feel there's more to you than meets the eye."

Meaning he wants to take my clothes off. "I'm a very ordinary person. Not at all your type," she said primly.

He laughed. "How do you know what my type is? As for ordinary, *weird* might be closer to the mark. Weird and moody."

"I'm not moody at all," she said unequivocally.

"No?" He cocked an eyebrow. "Then how come you were nice and friendly yesterday, but today you're as prickly as a porcupine?"

Because yesterday she hadn't known that he was the type who took advantage of innocent young women. However, she wasn't going to risk getting into an argument. He was probably the type of man who would think nothing of abandoning her on some rock if she annoyed him. In an attempt to change the subject, she indicated a flock of birds skimming the waves. "What are those?"

"Gulls, sweetie." His voice was light with laughter. "It's a bit early, but I think it's time I gave you some lunch—you're getting punchy."

She refused to be charmed by him. "I'm fine. I just don't have your expertise when it comes to birds."

"It doesn't take much expertise to recognize a gull."

"Not for you, perhaps, but I have other things on my mind."

"Really?" He raised an interrogative eyebrow. "Such as?"

She could have bitten out her tongue. "Private...problems."

"You're not married, by any chance?"

"It has nothing to do with men," she informed him loftily, although in point of fact it had everything to do with men. More and more she was beginning to think all problems were connected with the opposite sex. Maisy's unhappiness, the woman who'd been unceremoniously shipped off to Toronto... Everything had started because of some cheating man.

They landed in a small cove farther up the coast. Danny cut the motor, and the dory ground onto the shore with a crunch of pebbles.

Selby looked around anxiously, dismayed at the loneliness of this particular spot. "Are...are there any villages around here?" she asked.

"Nope. You can only get here by boat." He surveyed the cove fondly. "It's one of my favorite spots. It's a great place for observing wildlife, and it's sheltered from the wind."

One of his favorite spots to bring women he intended to make love to, no doubt. Well, he was in for a surprise. She'd taken judo....

She stood up, balancing carefully, and made to climb out of the dory. "Wait a minute," said Danny, who was in the water, pulling the boat farther up onto shore. "You'll get wet."

"I can manage," she insisted, stepping onto the seat.

He gave the boat an extra tug and she nearly fell into the sea. He caught her by the shoulders. "Easy does it, sweetheart!"

"I'd be fine if you'd stop jerking on the line," she complained. She could feel the strength of his fingers through her jacket. "You don't have to hold me."

"You can't get to shore by yourself," he explained. "I'll carry you."

"I can make it to shore," she said firmly. She didn't want him laying his hands on her. Not for *any* reason. "I'm wearing sneakers today, not boots."

"You need waders for this sea." And, ignoring her feeble cry of protest, he lifted her out of the dory in one rapid movement.

Involuntarily she cried out, "No!" but it was too late to object.

The pebbles made it difficult for him to walk, and so she was forced to cling to him, her arms wrapped unwillingly around his neck.

"Take it easy," he said, mistaking her aversion for fear. "I won't drop you." His face was close to hers, his skin cool against her cheek. She could feel the roughness of his beard, see the way his hair grew at the back of his neck. . . .

"That water's cold," he said when they were on the beach. "Your feet would have fallen off."

"You can put me down now."

Her voice was none too steady. For a moment she thought he was going to kiss her, and some perverse, crazy part of her *wanted* him to bring his mouth down on hers and kiss her until she swooned with pleasure. . . .

But he didn't kiss her. He simply set her gently down on the shingle and stroked a strand of wet hair away from her cheek.

"I'll get the stuff from the boat," he said. "Won't be a minute."

He brought a tarpaulin and spread it on the stones for them to sit on, then went back to the boat for the picnic cooler. She eyed the tarpaulin as suspiciously as if it had been a double bed. She was still eyeing it when he came back from the boat.

"Here we are." He put the cooler down. "Lunch! You want a beer?" She shook her head. "Well, there's coffee. I put the milk in a separate jar." He brought out a plastic box and opened it. "Two kinds of sandwiches, chicken or lobster, apples and cookies. We won't starve." He snapped the tab from a can of beer and took a thirsty swallow before adding, "My mother brought me up to believe it was discourteous to sit while a lady was standing. Or do you prefer to eat standing up?"

She didn't sit right away, and when she did it was as far away from him as she could get.

He looked at her inquiringly. "Would you rather I ate in the dory?" She moved a couple of inches closer. "Well, if Muhammad won't come to the mountain..." He seated himself next to her and put the picnic cooler between them. "For your peace of mind," he explained, "since being close seems to upset you."

He poured coffee into a plastic cup and handed it to her. It smelled surprisingly good, and she realized she was starving. "Did you say lobster?" she asked.

He nodded, a hank of black hair falling over his bony forehead. "From one of Mac's lobster pots. The mayonnaise is my contribution."

"Is Mac a lobster fisherman?"

"He's everything he can be to scrape out a living," Danny told her. "He puts down lobster pots, jigs for cod and does carpentry during the winter. There's also the store. Between them they manage."

"Lori told me they have a daughter in university," she said. "That must be a drain on them financially."

"Mmm," he mumbled through a mouthful of sandwich. Did she imagine it, or was his expression suddenly furtive?

Now what? she thought. Was Shari another young woman he'd lusted after? Perhaps her parents had shipped her off to university to get her away from him. She looked at him suspiciously over her lobster sandwich.

"You're doing it again," he said, dispatching the rest of his beer in one gulp. "You're looking at me as if I'm something particulary repellent that the tide washed up."

"That sounds like a guilty conscience to me," she said austerely.

He grinned. "My conscience is as clear as the driven snow. What about yours?"

She licked mayonnaise from her fingers. "What *about* mine?"

"Well, sweetheart, for all I know there may be a husband and children pining for you back in England."

"No husband. No children," she said.

"No lovers?"

"Not at the moment." She'd had men in her life, including one hasty—and disastrous—engagement, but since Maisy's illness, any men she'd been interested in had drifted away, and after her grandmother had died, Selby had been so obsessed with finding Daniel Forest that she hadn't really noticed that they'd gone.

"What about the rest of your family?" he persisted. "Do you have any sisters or brothers?"

"No. But I have friends." Yet in spite of her friends, she felt very alone in the world now that Maisy had left it.

"But nobody special?"

"All my friends are special." She rubbed an apple briskly on her sleeve. "Now it's my turn to do the cross-examining. Are you attached to anybody?"

"There was somebody in my life for a time," he said.

That must be the one who'd borne his child. "Are you going to marry her?"

He seemed surprised, and then he said in a voice as hard as steel, "No. No, I am not."

He looked so callous, so unyielding, that anger spurted in her like sudden flame. "You don't give a damn, do you?" she said, her voice uncomfortably shrill. "You don't give a damn about her."

He looked at her, his eyes hooded, and drawled, "Not anymore. No."

Selby thought about that poor abandoned young woman, and about Maisy, who had been so terribly betrayed by the other, older Danny, and something snapped inside her. She hurled the only thing that was to hand.

"You bastard!" The apple missed him and went rolling down the beach. "You heartless, unprincipled bastard!" And then, because she couldn't seem to stop, she went on shouting, "Bastard. Rotten, heartless bastard!" Her voice was as strident as a trumpet in the peaceful morning air.

CHAPTER FIVE

"IF YOU DON'T STOP screaming, I'll leave you here." Danny spoke softly, but the threat in his voice was unmistakable, and she stopped with a gulp.

He went and picked up the apple. "Fruit's expensive in Newfoundland. Next time you feel like braining me, use a stone."

Selby's rage had left her, but now she was shaking so hard she could hardly breathe. She was also more than a little frightened.

She must have been mad to attack him like that, but his casual dismissal of that poor girl had stirred too many ghosts, and she had really been yelling insults for Maisy's sake.

"There isn't a stone on the beach big enough for the job," she said, her soft lips set. "A man who treats women the way you do..."

He looked at her coldly. "Did Beth send you to hound me? Is this another of her little games?"

"I've not met her," she said, "but I know enough to know you've behaved like a bastard."

"So you said before. Or perhaps screeched would be a better description."

"You deserve to be screeched at. Somebody has to tell you what a louse you are."

"Maybe it's different in England," he said coldly, "but in this country you're told what the offense is before people hurl abuse at you."

She was suddenly sick of him, sick of the whole business. Depressed, too, because yesterday she'd been drawn to him. She'd found him attractive. To be honest, she still did, and this annoyed her, for how could one go on being attracted to a man who didn't possess an ounce of human decency?

"I want to go back to Savage Harbour, please," she said. "Now."

He gave her a look that could have withered fruit and started to thrust food back into the cooler. "You must be deranged," he said. "Either that, or Beth's using you as a go-between. It's the only possible excuse for your behavior."

"I don't want to discuss it anymore." She stared firmly at the horizon.

"Terrific! You scream at me like a fishwife, then clam up when I ask you why." He flung the cooler, followed by the tarpaulin, into the boat, then stood, looking at her balefully. "Come on, if you're coming!"

This time he didn't carry her to the dory. She had to wade. He had been right; the water was so cold her flesh seemed to shrivel on the bone, every scrap of feeling disappearing from her knees down.

She had scarcely taken her seat when he started the outboard and roared away at top speed, his face as set as the cliffs they were leaving behind. She sat huddled in the bow, hanging on for dear life, blinking icy spray out of her eyes, as they banged against the waves. This trip he didn't ask her if she felt seasick. If she'd felt sick as a dog, he clearly couldn't have cared less. If she'd fallen overboard, he would probably have cheered.

Only when they came into Savage Harbour did he reduce speed, and by this time Selby was drenched and shivering. He tied up the boat at the small stone wharf, and she staggered ashore, unable to feel the ground beneath her frozen feet.

"That was quite an experience," she said through chattering teeth. "However, I'm sure you'll understand if I don't thank you for it."

He stood up from tying the lines and looked at her with loathing. "I want you to get one thing straight, lady." He pointed a long finger at her. "I don't want you coming near me again while you're in Savage Harbour. Understand? I don't know what you and Beth are up to, but whatever it is, you're wasting your time. Now get lost, before I forget myself and toss you into the sea."

If she hadn't been so cold and wet, she would have argued, would have shouted at him that she'd never met Beth, but that as a woman she felt allied with her. But talking to this man was about as productive as talking to a dead fish, so she simply muttered childishly, "I certainly don't want to come near you. I'm particular," then tottered off to the store.

Lori was sitting at the counter reading a magazine when Selby came in, nearly falling over Barkis, who was blocking the doorway in her anxiety to get to her master. "Go to him, then," Selby grunted, holding the door open so that the animal could escape. "Better you than me."

"Been swimmin'?" asked Lori over the top of her magazine.

"I might as well have." The warmth of the store was like walking into a sauna, but she still couldn't stop shivering. "Is there hot water for a bath?"

"Sure is. When I fix a boiler, I don't fool around," Lori boasted. "When you're through, come on down an' we'll have a coffee."

Up in her room Selby dropped her jacket on the floor and peeled off her sneakers and socks. She was so cold it might have been the dead of winter, not September, and she cursed Danny as she rubbed her numb feet, trying to get the circulation going.

The hot bath helped, and she wallowed in it, washing the salt out of her hair, enjoying the tingling in her limbs as the blood slowly started to flow again. When she'd scrubbed herself till she was glowing, she added more hot water and lay back, trying to figure out what to do next.

There didn't seem much point in hanging around Savage Harbour. Avoiding Danny in a place this size wasn't possible, and she didn't fancy lurking in her room to stay out of his way. That meant she couldn't write the article she'd planned. But Savage Harbour wasn't the only fishing village in Newfoundland; she could always move on.

Another village. Of course! The brain wave hit her like a sledgehammer. She'd do an article on Beth. She'd go to her village and find out firsthand how the people there viewed the whole business. Then she'd fly to Toronto for an interview with the young woman herself. There was time before Mr. Forest returned from his vacation, and it would be worth it. Not only would she be striking a blow for women, it would make a super article. A girl, pregnant, rejected by her lover, banished from her home, family and friends...

She got out of the tub and vigorously toweled herself until her neat little body was the same shade as a freshly cooked lobster. She'd show the Danny Forests of this world. Her story might not make world headlines, but it might make men like him think a bit before fooling innocent young women.

Back in the store, she seated herself at the counter and accepted the mug of coffee Lori handed her. Now all she had to do was find out which village Beth had lived in. She had to do it tactfully and not give away what she was up to, since Lori and her husband appeared to view Danny as a cross between Superman and the Pope.

It was easier to broach the subject than she'd imagined, because when Lori asked her why Danny had come back in such a hurry, Selby told her he had been angry.

"Yeah?" Lori looked interested. "Did Wilf send him on a wild-goose chase?"

"No," replied Selby, "it wasn't because of Wilf." She poured cream into her coffee. "We'd been talking about a girl he'd known. A girl in the next village. She'd had a baby, and he got mad when I said I thought he'd behaved badly."

"Badly!" Lori looked startled. "What the heck did he tell you?"

"Not much. Just her name, and—"

"I'm surprised he mentioned her," Lori mused. "It ain't like Danny to boast."

"Boast!" Strange ethics Lori had. "I can't see that ruining a young woman's life is a reason to boast."

"Ruinin'? What are you talkin' about?" Lori was indignant. "Danny saved her life, that's all."

"Saved her *life?*" echoed Selby.

"Yeah! We all told her Len Crowchuck weren't no good, an' him a married man an' all, but she wouldn't listen. Well, you know how it is."

Selby felt herself grow weak. "You...you mean Danny isn't the father?"

"Danny?" Lori's mouth gaped. "Are you nuts? *Danny?*"

"Oh, lor!" Selby said weakly. "Oh, lor! I think I've made a big mistake."

"I should think you have." Lori looked grim. "Accusin' Danny of such a thing."

"It was a misunderstanding," Selby pleaded. "I jumped to conclusions."

"You should be more careful," Lori scolded. "You could get yourself prosecuted."

She looked so disapproving Selby was afraid she wouldn't talk to her anymore. "You're right, I've been an idiot." She gave a weak grin. "It wouldn't be the first time."

"Danny, indeed," grumbled Lori. "You oughta be ashamed."

"I am," Selby said contritely. "But please, Lori, set me straight. This Len character. He's the father?"

"Who else? Always been a ladies' man, has Len, and always liked 'em young, and Marni Roberts never had much sense—"

"Marni Roberts? Who's that?"

"The girl who had Len's baby, of course."

"Then . . . who's Beth?" asked Selby, thoroughly confused.

"Who?"

"Danny kept mentioning someone called Beth."

"There ain't no one called Beth around here," said Lori. "The name don't mean nothin' to me."

"I know he said 'Beth,'" insisted Selby. "I know that."

"Well, it must be one of his women back in Halifax. Danny's attractive to women. I reckon there's always a woman on the scene."

"I'm between someones," he'd said, implying there was a steady stream of females in his life, and the stab of jealousy she felt was both unwarranted and foolish.

"Anyway," Lori continued, "when Marni told her parents she was pregnant they turned her out. They always was as cold as charity—a lot of churchgoin' but no real Christian feelin', know what I mean?"

Selby nodded. "So we took her in," Lori went on.

"You mean you and Mac?"

"Ain't I tellin' you? She moved into Shari's room, where you are now. But she never stopped cryin', she was that ashamed, poor kid, an' she was still crazy about Len." Lori made a face. "Can't understand it meself. I'd've gone after him with a rollin' pin."

"But how does Danny fit into this?"

"Well, Danny's over here all the time, an' he gets to meet her, an' he talks to her, an' she gets to trust him. In the end he's just about the only person she does trust, an' she tells him she's gonna get rid of the baby by takin' some pills one of her girlfriends give her, an' if they didn't work, God knows what else she was gonna try."

"You mean . . . ?"

Lori nodded. "She was that desperate, poor little cow, she might have done anything."

"Poor girl," said Selby. "Thank God she had you and Mac."

"An' Danny!" said Lori sharply.

"And Danny. Yes." She took a sip of coffee. "What did he do?"

Lori grinned reminiscently. "First he flushed them pills down the toilet, and then he arranged for her to go to Toronto, to some place for teenage mothers where she'll have good care an' where they'll help her decide what she wants to do when the baby comes. He paid for it all, an' when she decided to keep the little girl, he offers to go on helpin' her so's she can go back to school an' in time make a decent life for herself an' the kid."

"Danny did that? He didn't just ship her away?" The ice that had clutched at Selby's soul since last night started to melt away.

"He saved her life, I'm tellin' you," repeated Lori firmly.

Selby jumped up and ran for the door, nearly knocking a stand of sunglasses over in her haste.

"What's got into you now?" Lori called after her.

"I've got to find Danny," she called back. "I've got to repair some fences."

She had done him a terrible injustice. How many times had Maisy warned her that her impulsiveness would land her in trouble? But she never seemed to learn, and now she'd done it again, and she had to put it right.

She started for the lighthouse, then spied him on the little shingle beach collecting seaweed from the rocky low-water line. She ran down toward him, her feet skidding on the loose stones, her heart-shaped face alight with purpose.

He straightened up, looked at her through narrowed unfriendly eyes and said shortly, "I told you to keep away."

"I have to talk to you." Her mouth was as dry as charcoal.

"Why? Have you thought up some more names?"

"Please, Danny!"

"Well, I don't want to talk to you." He scowled down at Barkis, who, recognizing a friend, was attempting to lick Selby's hand.

"*Please,* Danny."

"Either you have the hide of a rhinoceros or you're very stupid," he said coldly. "I thought I made it clear that I don't want you near me."

"Yes, but—"

He said with a deliberation generated by anger, "I don't want you near me. I don't want to talk to you."

"I don't care whether you want to or not!" she returned, her voice rising. "I've got something to say."

Several fishermen on the quay stopped mending their nets and looked down at them with interest.

"Get lost, lady," Danny said through gritted teeth.

"If you'd just *listen* to me—"

"I've already listened to you, and I didn't like what I heard."

He started to walk away, and she clutched at his sleeve. "Will you listen—"

"You're too much!" he said, shaking her off. "Too bloody much! You call me every name you can lay your tongue on one minute, and the next you come prancing down here and expect me to welcome you with open arms...."

"I don't expect that," she bellowed. "I just want—"

"Get away from me, Selby," he said with chilling ferocity. "Far, far away."

"Will you *listen*!" She was close to tears of frustration. "I want to *apologize*."

He gave her a look like an armed camp. "Apology accepted. Now, get going."

"You s-stubborn, p-pigheaded..." she stuttered, her frustration getting the better of her.

He gave a mirthless grin. "That's more in character."

"I've admitted I was in the wrong," she snarled. "At least let me explain."

"What's happened? Have you been on the phone to Beth? Have the two of you cooked up some new scheme?"

"Oh, God! You're paranoid about this Beth woman."

"With good reason."

"I've never *met* her, I tell you." He started to walk away again and she called after him. "I got her muddled up with Marni Roberts."

"Marni Roberts?" He turned back. "What's Marni Roberts got to do with it?"

"Everything." She took a deep breath. "I thought you were the father of her baby."

The fishermen leaned farther over the edge of the quay.

"Perhaps we'd better discuss this somewhere else," said Danny. "I'm not wild about turning this into a soap opera for the locals."

He strode up the beach and walked over to his station wagon. Selby stumbled after him.

"Let's take a drive," he said.

"You sound like a Mafia godfather," said Selby with a giggle. She tended to make bad jokes when she was nervous.

"Get in!" he barked, clearly not amused.

He drove along the coast for about two miles without speaking. Selby made a couple of remarks about the view, but he ignored her, so she fell silent, too. Only Barkis, sitting in the back, seemed at ease. She pushed her snout into Selby's neck and gave an occasional whine of impatience.

"Good dog. Good girl," said Selby, thinking that if only she could pat Danny the same way and make things right between them, life would be a great deal easier than it was. Danny parked at a lookout high on a cliff above an inlet. He got out, and Selby followed. Below them the waves surged and retreated. The wind tore at them, raking their hair, whipping the color into their cheeks. Excited by its boisterous play, Barkis started running in circles over the short grass, yelping joyously.

Danny leant against the guardrail. On either side great walls of granite stretched as far as the eye could see. Small birds, their wings whirring like clockwork, flew overhead.

"What are they?" asked Selby, hoping that this interest in wildlife might soften his heart.

Danny barely glanced at them. "Atlantic puffins," he said. She noticed the fine web of lines around his eyes that must have come from squinting into the sun. It made him look older than his twenty-nine years, and was definitely sexy.

"They're so little," she babbled. "I always thought puffins were big birds. Are we disturbing their nests?" She didn't really give a damn about their nests, but she felt compelled to fill the difficult silence.

"They only nest on the cliffs during summer," he said. "They winter offshore." He turned so that the sun shone on his face, gilding its hard contours, emphasizing the lines that bracketed his mouth. Selby thought, *It's true he's not handsome, but he is attractive, dammit. He's as attractive as the devil.*

"Now then, Selby," the attractive devil said tersely, "what's been going on?"

She crossed her arms in front of her, hugging her elbows. "I want to apologize."

"You've already done that," he said, his eyes gleaming coldly. "Now I want to know what prompted your extraordinary behavior."

"It's hard to know where to start," she said, looking at the tossing, wind-whipped sea.

"You might start by telling me where you got the insane idea that I'd fathered poor little Marni's baby."

"It was something I heard Mac and Lori talking about. Something..." She faltered to a stop.

His eyes were black ice. "Mac and Lori told you—"

"No! No, of course not. It was something I...I overheard."

"Listening at doors, were you?"

She couldn't look at him. "Yes. I know it's awful, but...but I'd run out of toothpaste—"

"Toothpaste!" His lips twisted sardonically. "Of course, that explains everything."

She took a deep breath and plunged on. "They were talking about this girl and...and they didn't know I was behind the door...listening."

"Eavesdropping."

She winced. "I suppose it must seem like that."

"It *was* like that, sweetheart."

She lifted her head. A mixture of shame and the wind had turned her normally pale cheeks bright pink. "I'm not proud of myself," she said, her voice level again. "I behaved badly. I know I did. I'm just trying to tell you how it happened." He didn't reply, and she added, "I don't usually listen at doors, nor do I attack people with apples, if it comes to that."

He gave the ghost of a smile. "It could have been worse. You could have gone for me with the anchor."

Her heart lifted just a little. His face was still stern, but she sensed that his anger was abating. "I really am sorry," she said. "I do tend to...fly off on tangents, and when I heard Lori say you'd sent this girl to Toronto, I just...assumed that you'd done it because you were the father of her baby and you wanted her out of the way."

"Do Lori and Mac know you overheard them?"

"Heavens, no! They don't even know I came downstairs again last night."

"What I don't understand," said Danny, "is why you didn't bawl me out right away? Why wait till lunchtime to start throwing fruit at me?"

"Well..." This was tricky. "I was, er, afraid if I didn't come with you, you'd...you'd take Beverly, and..."

"You wanted to protect her from my advances."

"Er, something like that," she admitted, biting her lip.

"Thanks a lot!"

"I didn't know what to do," she said helplessly. "And then on the beach this morning when you talked about Beth, I thought you meant Marni. I mean, I didn't discover that Marni *wasn't* Beth until I talked to Lori later."

"You've lost me temporarily," he said, shaking his head. "Am I right in assuming you did talk to Lori?"

"When we got back this afternoon."

"And she put you straight?"

She nodded. "Yes. She was pretty mad."

"I think you need a keeper," he said quietly. "You're not safe out on your own. Do you always jump to such wild conclusions?"

"Not always." Honesty made her add, "But more often than I should."

"It must play havoc with your work."

"I always double-check the facts when I'm writing a story." Past experience and a firm editor had taught her that.

"I guess it's nice you're so resolutely on the side of women and fair play," he said dryly, "but just for the record, so am I."

"I know that now," she said, "and I think that what you did for Marni was terrific."

He held up his hand. "Cut it out, Selby. I just happened to be at the right place at the right time, that's all. It's no big deal. And I *don't* want people knowing about it. Understood?"

"Understood."

"Apart from anything else, it wouldn't be fair to Marni."

He loomed so tall above her she had to tilt her head to look into his face. "I won't make any more trouble, I promise," she said, thinking guiltily, *Until the time comes to confront your grandfather.*

He put his hand under her chin, and the touch of his fingers sent a little shock down to her toes. "You need watching," he said, "and I'd like to be the guy to do it." Then he kissed her gently on the mouth.

It was as if she'd been waiting all her life for this. That with him there was safety, possibly love....

Had she gone insane? She was at it again. Leaping without looking first. Getting herself into something she wasn't going to be able to handle.

It was a brief kiss, consoling rather than passion-
ate, and when it was finished, he cupped her face in his
hands. "Next time, when something's troubling you,
talk to me before you blow your stack, okay?"

"Okay," she said, staring at him from troubled gray
eyes.

He kissed the tip of her nose and then each eyelid.
"You're crazy, you know that? Crazy as a loon."

She smiled sheepishly. "I suppose it must look that
way."

"You'd better believe it, sweetheart," he said, giving her a little hug before letting her go. Barkis came
up and flopped down at his feet, tongue lolling.

"Ready to go home, girl?" He patted the dog's
back. "Want your dinner?" At the magic word Barkis got up and started whining.

"As penance, how about joining me in the lighthouse for dinner tonight?" Danny said as they walked
back to the station wagon.

"Is your cooking *that* bad?" Selby smiled. The
feeling between them was warm again, and even
though she knew it was unwise, she couldn't hold back
the happiness that swept over her, like the sea sweeping over the rocks below.

"I'll have you know I'm well-known for my
steaks," he said.

"Because they're good or because they're awful?"

"Why not come and find out for yourself?"

"I'd love to. Besides, steak will be a nice change
from fish."

"Ah, well!" said Danny, holding the door of the station wagon open for her. "If you can't tame 'em with kindness, tame 'em with food."

"Is that what you want to do?" she asked after she climbed in. "Tame me?"

He turned in the driver's seat. "As a matter of fact, whenever I'm with you, I feel I want to look after you," he said. "When I'm not wanting to murder you, that is."

"Subjugation and murder! Sounds like a great beginning to friendship," she replied lightly. But his sympathy disturbed her. Since Maisy's death, sympathy was something she found hard to deal with.

And he disturbed her still more when he murmured, "I guess friendship will have to do for the time being, but soon I hope we'll mean more to each other than just friends. Much, much more."

CHAPTER SIX

THE STEAKS WERE THICK and tender, and Danny served baked potatoes with them, which was a nice change from fries.

"You'll have to make do with tinned hearts of palm for salad," he said. "Lettuce isn't readily available here—they don't have the soil for it."

Selby took a sip of red wine. Danny only had juice glasses at the lighthouse, but the wine they drank was a fine Saint Emilion, as smooth and rich on the tongue as cream. "Why don't you start a hydroponic garden?" she suggested. "I did an article last year on hydroponic gardening. It's amazing what you can grow."

She looked across at him enthusiastically, her bright eyes framed by lashes that curled like the petals of a flower. She was enjoying herself enormously. It must be the wine, she thought, putting down her glass. She'd better go easy.

"Why not come over next year? You could help me start one." He smiled and her bones seemed to turn to jelly. "We could spend a hydroponic summer in Savage Harbour."

"Sounds a bit damp to me. Besides, I'm a working girl. I can't take the summer off whenever I feel like it." *Oh, but it would be fun to spend the summer here with Danny. Impossible, of course, but fun.*

"Neither can I, sweetheart," he said, pouring them both more wine. "You forget, I have a business to run."

She giggled. "You don't seem to be doing much of that at the moment."

He pushed back the sleeve of his sweater to look at the calendar on his wristwatch, and she repressed a desire to stroke the sprinkling of dark hairs on his tanned wrist, to feel his warm flesh....

"I'm due back in my office in precisely three days, twelve hours and forty-five minutes. Until then I'm on holiday and—" he smiled at her again "—at your disposal."

"Well, I do have to write that article." Her heart was giving great leaps of pleasure, like a gazelle gone mad.

"Well, I could help," he insisted. "Give you local color. Besides, it won't take all your time, will it?"

"N-no...." He was taking her over again, and part of her liked it and part of her didn't. For safety's sake she decided to concentrate on the part that didn't.

"We could visit the Devil's Punchbowl, and then there's Cogan's Heath...."

"We'll see," she said, "but I'm a slow writer." In reality she wrote at breakneck speed, the way she made decisions, but she'd need a plausible excuse if he started pressuring her. To change the drift of the conversation, she asked him, "Are you the only member of your family who works in the family business?"

"Not entirely. Dad's a corporate lawyer and he's retained by the firm. But my younger brother isn't interested in the business, and Granddad retired when I graduated from university."

"So you're the big boss."

Danny took their empty plates over to the sink. "I try to be, but it's not easy when Granddad's around. He's used to running things," he told her, putting a wooden platter of cheeses onto the table and going back to the cupboard for crackers. "And so am I. It can lead to arguments."

She cut slices of cheese for them both. "Don't you get along with your grandfather, then?"

"We get along just fine, but we're *both* stubborn as hell." He pulled a face. "I'm told we're alike."

If that was the case, she could understand Maisy's falling in love so quickly. But she was going to make damn sure the same thing didn't happen to her.

The talk drifted to the rest of his family. He had a married sister living in Calgary, his younger brother was studying computer science at Queen's University in Ontario, and his mother wrote a gardening column for a local newspaper. "She's a gardening nut," Danny said. "She'll probably be arrested at the airport for trying to smuggle in cuttings of European plants."

Maisy had loved gardening, too, but, unlike the privileged family who had turned their backs on her, her circumstances hadn't allowed much scope for her hobby.

Selby, remembering why she was really here in Canada, got up abruptly. "I'll do the washing-up," she said, "and then I must go."

"Go! Where?" He rose, too. "I thought dinner and a movie..."

"Beverly will be waiting for you to help her with her homework," Selby said tartly.

"I think she has to start doing her homework on her own. I'll be gone soon. And besides—" his rich brown eyes grew serious "—she's becoming infatuated with me. It's not fair to the child to encourage her."

So he had noticed, and more important, he didn't intend to encourage her for the sake of his vanity. It was a point in his favor, and she relaxed a little. "What movie did you have in mind? And how far do we have to go to see it?"

He pointed a long finger up to the ceiling. "One floor up. And the choice is yours. I have quite a library of films."

"Do you have *Casablanca*?" Selby particularly loved the old classic films, and when he nodded she was sorely tempted.

"This theater also serves coffee during the movie," he added, noticing her hesitation, "*and* I'll stop the film and replay any part you want to see twice."

"Well—" she shrugged her shoulders in mock defeat "—how can I refuse? But first we should do the washing-up."

He reached over and ruffled her hair. "The dishes can wait," he said. "Bogart can't. Let's go."

Perhaps *Casablanca* wasn't the ideal film to watch with a man you're attracted to but have decided to keep at arm's length. The love scenes between Bogart and Bergman seemed more poignant than Selby remembered them, the music more bittersweet; always prone to crying at the movies, she felt the tears well up and slide relentlessly down her smooth cheeks.

"Here." Danny put the film on hold and plonked a large box of man-size tissues on the table in front of them. "I like to give a girl a good time, but aren't you rather overdoing it?"

"Oh! I do feel such a fool," she said, blowing her nose into a tissue. She knew that it wasn't only *Casablanca* that had released this flood. Months of pent-up emotions were spilling over, and now she couldn't seem to stop.

"You're not a fool, Selby, and you're among friends." He put an arm around her shoulders and held her close, soothing her gently, as if she were a frightened child. "Shh, shh, sweetheart, it's okay."

"I d-don't know what's come over me...." She gulped, mopping her streaming eyes.

He smoothed a strand of hair off her wet cheeks. His eyes, which had seemed as hard as flint earlier, were now as soft as velvet. "As long as it's not my cooking...."

She smiled mistily. "It's not indigestion, I promise."

"That's all right, then," he said, and gently brought his lips down onto her trembling ones.

It was a tender kiss, comforting and undemanding—and it was Selby's undoing.

She gave a fluttery little sigh and abandoned herself to an unfamiliar languorous pleasure. Deep, deep inside her, desire stirred faintly, and she wound her arms around his neck and pressed herself closer.

"You know, you're lovely," he whispered huskily. "Swollen eyes and all."

She snuggled against him, throwing all caution to the winds, and he kissed her again, ardently this time, and a wave of lust rippled through her. She arched against him like an amorous cat.

Barkis leaned her beige muzzle on Selby's knee and gave a low growl of jealousy. At first Selby was too engrossed to notice, then Barkis's growl grew deeper.

Sanity reasserted itself. Selby pulled herself upright. "It's all right, Barkis," she croaked. "It's all right. Good dog."

"Damn interfering dog, more like it," Danny said, grabbing his pet by the collar. "I'd forgotten how possessive she is. I'll put her downstairs. Don't go away, sweetheart."

"No!" Selby blurted. He stopped pulling the reluctant dog.

"No?" he repeated, his eyebrows raised.

"Please, Danny," she said, pulling down her blue sweater and sitting up very straight in the love seat. "Please understand. *Please*. Everything's happening too fast, and I..." She stopped, her eyes shadowed by tears and doubt.

"It's all right, sweetheart," he said. "I understand."

But he didn't. How could he? How could he know she was terrified of the past repeating itself?

When he let Barkis go, the dog gave him a reproachful look and went to sit beside Selby, just to show him.

"I think we ought to give the rest of *Casablanca* a miss, though, don't you?" said Danny. "Otherwise I'll have to put on my wet suit. How about the Marx Brothers? They don't make you cry, do they?"

"I feel like a comedy act myself," she said wryly. "I *am* a fool!"

"Perhaps. But your whacky charm more than makes up for it."

She smiled again. "Thanks a lot!"

"My pleasure," he replied, bowing.

They spent the rest of the evening watching the Marx Brothers, Danny's arm around Selby's shoulders, Barkis lying over their feet, and gradually, when she realized he wasn't going to try kissing her again, she relaxed and gave her attention to the movie and the antics of the four zany brothers. Outside the store he kissed her good-night. A quick, friendly kiss, but the brief touch of his lips still sent a tingle down her spine, and she felt a pang because she wouldn't be staying with him in his cozy lighthouse, where the only view from the bedroom window was of the limitless ocean.

"I'll leave you alone in the morning to work in peace," he said, "on the understanding that we spend the rest of the day together. Is that okay?"

"It sounds very fair,' she agreed.

"Oh, I can be very sensible—if it means getting what I want." He smiled. "And I want to spend time with you very much indeed."

The next three days flew by. The weather held, and every afternoon Danny collected her and they went off together. He showed her the Devil's Punchbowl, they picked late blueberries on Cogan's Heath and visited other coves and villages, collecting data for Selby's article.

On the last evening Danny took her to visit some friends of his who lived farther down the coast. "Do your friends live in a lighthouse, too?" she asked on the drive to their place.

"I'm the only lighthouse dweller around these parts," Danny said. "The Merrills live in an old house that was built for a whaling captain."

"An old house—it sounds very grand."

She wished she'd put on a skirt rather than her tan slacks and sweater. Not that Danny was exactly dressed up, in his black turtleneck and worn gray corduroys, but he wore his clothes with such easy grace he would look elegant wearing a barrel.

"Well, not old by British standards, I guess," he amended. "It was built in the eighteenth century. It was a total mess when Jim bought it. They've done wonders with it."

"I'm looking forward to seeing it," Selby said, although she hoped they'd spend their last evening together in the lighthouse, looking at movies perhaps, or just talking, because for the past two nights Danny had joined her for dinner at the store, and afterward they'd stayed on, playing cards or chatting with the other customers. Danny knew everybody, and he'd encouraged them to reminisce, so she'd managed to get a lot for her article, but it didn't offer much opportunity for kissing. A quick hug and a peck on the cheek had been the extent of their lovemaking since the night she'd cried over *Casablanca,* and although she shied away from admitting it, she was hungry for more.

They turned a bend and followed a smaller road that wound up toward a wood of stunted conifers. "There it is," said Danny, nodding at a tall stone house in the curve of a hill.

"It's certainly... different," Selby murmured, for it sprouted turrets, balconies and terraces in a most alarming way.

"It's got lots of room," Danny explained. "Lisa needs lots of room for her work."

"What does she do?"

"She's an artist. They both are."

He parked in front of the house, but they had no sooner climbed out of the car when the front door opened and a stocky man, his face partially hidden behind a red beard, hurled himself down the front steps.

"Danny, you old devil, we thought you'd forgotten us," he bellowed, throwing himself on Danny and giving him an exuberant hug. They made an incongruous couple—Danny, tall and elegant as a wolfhound, his friend short and chunky as a bulldog.

"It must be months since you honored us with a visit, you creep," Jim rattled on. "Lisa was beginning to get quite worried. We thought you'd drowned in that dory of yours or fallen off the top of your lighthouse."

"You can't get rid of me that easily." Danny laughed. "Now shut up for a minute, will you? I want to introduce you to Selby."

"Hi, Selby!" Jim took Selby's small hand in his large one. "You must be the girl Danny found on a rock. I must say, you're a sight more attractive than the stuff he usually finds."

"Don't talk about her as if she were a barnacle," Danny protested. "Aren't you going to invite us in? It's freezing out here."

"Sorry, sorry!" Jim led them inside, his solid arm around Selby's shoulders. "You must bear with me, Selby. I'm a lousy host—Lisa's always bawling me out about it. But I don't notice the cold, particularly when I see something beautiful. And that coloring of yours—so delicate, so subtle. I can't wait to capture it on paper."

"Can we can eat first?" Danny asked. "Or don't you notice hunger pangs either?"

"Peasant!" His friend grinned. "I'll have you know I've been cooking all day. Well, most of it—had to do some work on my new floral piece—but of course we're going to eat. We asked you for dinner, didn't we?" He shot a friendly glare in Danny's direction. "What do you take me for?"

"I take you for a certifiable nut," said Danny, "and poor Selby's probably kicking herself for agreeing to come."

"I'm black-and-blue," said Selby, who was beginning to enjoy herself.

Jim looked contrite. "I do come on a bit strong sometimes," he admitted. "Lisa's always telling me to calm down—"

Danny cut in. "Where is Lisa, anyway?"

"In the kitchen. You'll like Lisa," Jim assured Selby. "She's quiet."

He led them through a bare hall littered with hunks of torn pieces of metal. There were no mirrors or any paintings on the walls, nor was there a stick of furniture or an ornament in sight. The effect was one of total bleakness, and Selby was beginning to wonder if the Merrills were squatters in this huge barn of a house.

"Here we are!" announced Jim, letting go of Selby's shoulders and opening a door at the end of the passage. "Home at last!"

Selby stood on the threshold, her gray eyes wide with surprise. The contrast with the hall couldn't have been greater. It was a huge kitchen, with high ceilings that swam with shadows and glittered with light from tall, narrow windows. A handsome Welsh dresser loaded with blue-and-white china stood against one wall. Sea-worn stones and shells and beach glass were spread on a polished oak chest, and brass and pewter gleamed in the glow of a blazing fire.

In the center of the room, a long table covered with a gaily colored Indian bedspread was set for four.

"It's lovely," Selby blurted. "Just lovely!"

"Surprise, surprise," said Danny with a knowing grin.

A plump little butterball of a woman bounded up from one of two enormous sofas that flanked the fireplace, scattering cats in all directions. "Danny!" she said. "We've missed you."

Danny leaned down to kiss her cheek. "I've been busy, Lisa. So have you, I hope."

"I have indeed. Thanks to you." She squeezed his arm. For a little woman she had remarkably large hands.

"Lisa, look what Danny brought!" roared Jim, pulling Selby farther into the room. "Nice, eh?"

Danny said, "Selby, this is Lisa. The civilized partner of this ménage."

Lisa shook her head in resignation, saying, "You must forgive my husband. He means well, but he was never properly house-trained." Her face was too round for real prettiness, but she had fine clear skin, and eyes that shone like blue lamps when she smiled. "I'm glad you came to visit us, Selby. I get starved for civilized company sometimes."

Danny handed his host a paper bag containing a bottle. "Champagne!" boomed Jim, opening the bag and holding the bottle aloft. "What's this in aid of?"

Danny's eyes caught and held Selby's. "A glorious autumn, English visitor... Do we need an excuse to drink champagne?"

"None whatever," agreed Lisa, going to the Welsh dresser for glasses. "Let's have a glass now, shall we? To start the meal off with a sparkle."

They enjoyed a leisurely, hilarious meal, prepared and served by Jim. It was simple: a fish stew, home-made bread and butter, and a dish of sliced tomatoes and peppers. The good fellowship and good talk warmed the room as much as the fire did, and by the time they were eating Lisa's baked apples with cinnamon, Selby felt as comfortable with the Merrills as she did with any of her old friends back home.

They moved to the sofas to have their coffee in front of the fire, and when Danny put his arm around her, she leaned her head on his shoulder and felt happier than she had in all the time since her grandmother had died and left her with nothing but the thought of revenge to warm her empty heart.

Lisa leaned forward and put another log on the fire. "That was a great supper, Jimbo," she said. "Thank you."

His homely face glowed with pleasure. "It was no big deal. You provided half of it."

"I flung four apples into the oven!" She turned to Selby. "That's the extent of my culinary skills. I'm hopeless in the kitchen, but Jimbo's a genius. I don't know how I'd manage without him."

"You'd starve, honey," Jim said. "When she works she forgets to eat," he explained to Selby. "I have to drag her to the table by force."

Selby smiled, full and contented. "Are those your paintings?" she asked Lisa, nodding at one wall hung from floor to ceiling with delicate watercolors.

"Heavens, no," said Lisa. "Those are Jimbo's." They were mostly floral pieces, delicate as lace. It was hard to imagine stocky Jim Merrill doing anything so fragile. "I don't have his delicate touch," Lisa explained. "I'm a sculptor."

"She's a great sculptor!" Jim declared. "Her work makes my piddling little pictures look like trash."

"That's nonsense, Jimbo," Lisa said. "You're very talented. There just isn't the same market for watercolors, that's all."

"Lisa's the real artist in this household," Jim told Selby, his eyes shining with pride. "I just mess around."

"These don't look like messing around to me," Selby said, getting up and going over to examine the pictures. But she could see what he meant. His work was charming, pretty, but it lacked the force of serious art. "Are any of your pieces in here?" she asked Lisa.

"There isn't enough room for my stuff in here," said Lisa. "I tend to create large pieces. Would you like to come to the studio and take a look?"

"That's a compliment, Selby," Danny said. "Lisa doesn't usually invite people into her studio."

"But we don't want you along," Lisa said when the two men made to accompany them. "I don't want Selby distracted when she looks at my stuff."

Jim grinned. "What you mean is, you want us to do the dishes while you're away."

Lisa opened the door to the hall. "Great idea," she said. "There are clean dish towels in the middle drawer of the dresser."

"My studio's at the front of the house," she told Selby as they walked down the hall. "In fact, the rest of the house is just one big studio. We live in the kitchen and a couple of rooms above it."

"Do you work with local stone?" Selby asked.

"I don't work with stone anymore. I work with metal. I use scrap steel, mostly from wrecks when I can get hold of it. That's how I first met Danny. He'd been diving around a wreck I was interested in, and I phoned him to ask him about it. That was about five years ago now, and we've been friends ever since.''

They reached the end of the hall and Lisa rattled a doorknob impatiently. "Damn this catch, it always sticks. Ah!'' The heavy door swung open with a creak.

She pressed a switch and light flooded space the size of an airplane hangar.

"Wow!'' gasped Selby, looking up.

"We knocked out the ceilings to make space,'' Lisa explained. A vast metal shape seemed to take up the entire area, its sharp angles stretched up into the shadows of the ceiling, two winglike structures spreading from side to side.

"You don't have to pretend to like it,'' Lisa said as Selby walked slowly around the thing.

"It's a bird, isn't it?'' she asked finally.

Lisa nodded. "You got it! It's for Eagle Insurance in Montreal. My second commission. Danny got it for me.''

"Danny did?''

"Yep! He showed them the sculpture I did for his firm, and I suspect he twisted their arm a little. Frankly, it's saved our lives.'' Her blue eyes glowed. "He's the greatest, is Danny.''

Selby craned her head. "This is really good,'' she said. At first the enormous sculpture had daunted her, but now that she'd figured out the shape of the thing—the predatory beak and outstretched wings—she could tell it was a powerful piece of work. "Is it finished?''

"Pretty well. Next comes the boring part. I've got to scrub all the rust off it and coat it with weather-proof varnish." She moved a welder's mask off the cluttered bench to make room to sit down. "Too bad you won't be around to help. I'm recruiting my friends for that bit."

"I have to get back to Halifax. I'm just passing through," she said.

Lisa pulled at the silvery threads of her Indian skirt. "I wouldn't count on that if I were you."

"What do you mean?"

"Well, Danny seems really smitten—and I can see why." She looked up, smiling.

Selby smiled back. "You mean because of my dynamite personality?"

But Lisa seemed quite serious. "I mean because you seem so right together," she said. "It's almost as if you've known each other for years, or had some sort of family connection."

Selby felt herself grow faint. "We've only known each other a few days," she said mechanically, but Lisa's words had opened a gate she'd unconsciously kept shut.

Until now she'd refused to face the knowledge that indeed she and Danny had a strong family connection. They shared the same grandfather, which made them first cousins.

First cousins. Almost the same as brother and sister.

CHAPTER SEVEN

THE REMAINDER of the evening was spoiled for Selby. When they rejoined the men, she was silent, her mind churning like a cement mixer, her gray eyes troubled.

Her mind had plenty to churn about. She'd been so obsessed with the idea of vindicating Maisy that she had thought of the elder Daniel Forest only as seducer, betrayer, number-one rat fink, but never as her mother's father—her maternal grandfather! This was a new role he was playing in the drama, and one that affected her directly, because it meant that Danny was her first cousin, and weren't first cousins discouraged from mating? Selby had a hazy notion that it was genetically dangerous.

What's this about mating? asked a small, still voice inside her that sounded remarkably like Maisy's. *All you've done so far is kiss.*

So far, thought Selby, gazing into the fire. *But it's not going to stay at just kissing much longer, and marriage to my first cousin is out of the question.*

Marriage! hooted the inner voice. *There you go again. Jumping to conclusions like a demented flea! He hasn't even invited you into his bed, let alone proposed.*

But he will, Selby thought. *He will. And when he does it will break my heart to refuse him.*

Racked by these thoughts, she was unable to contribute much to the general conversation.

She fidgeted on her chair. "What's wrong, sweetheart?" Danny asked her. "You're very silent."

"The poor girl doesn't have much choice when you and Jim get going," Lisa said.

He reached out to smooth Selby's cheek with a knuckle, and she had to steel herself not to flinch at his touch. "Sure you're all right?" he said.

"I'm fine," she lied bravely.

He didn't look convinced, but let it go and turned away to continue his argument with Jim.

She felt weighed down by doubt and deceit. She couldn't escape the fact that she'd never told Danny her real reason for coming to Canada. And she hadn't been honest about the relationship between Maisy and his grandfather, either. She'd implied they were casual friends during the war, not lovers. She hadn't said anything about an illegitimate daughter and leaving Maisy in the lurch, and she hadn't even *thought* about being Danny's cousin.

She bucked in her chair and Danny looked over at her inquiringly. "Are you all right, Selby?"

"A cramp in my leg," she said, although a cramp in her conscience would have been nearer the truth.

"Try a glass of my parsnip wine—it's great for cramps," Jim suggested.

"A glass of your parsnip wine and one's whole body goes into a cramp," Danny said. "The stuff's lethal."

Selby smiled wanly. "I'll be fine. I'm a bit tired, that's all."

Danny got up, looking at his watch. "Why didn't you say so, sweetheart? It's late anyway. We're keeping these two up past their bedtime, and we should be making tracks."

On their way to the car Jim pressed a small, flat package into her hands. "Since we won't be seeing you again—a small remembrance. Don't open it now. Save it for later."

"Well, I don't believe we won't be seeing you again," Lisa declared, "and I have a feeling for such things, don't I, Jimbo?"

"She does," her husband affirmed. "Along with everything else, my talented wife is gifted with second sight."

"And I would stake my life that you'll be back within the year," Lisa added.

"If I do come back, I'll make a point of visiting you," Selby said, although she knew it was an empty promise.

"You'd better," said Danny. "I'll put a hex on you if you don't."

They laughed, but Selby's mirth was forced, because there *was* a hex on her already. An invincible one. A tie of blood she could no longer ignore.

Driving home in the car, Danny said, "I certainly hope you intend to prove Lisa right and come back soon, sweetheart."

"It's not quite that simple," she replied tightly. "I work for a living, and airfares are expensive."

"I could always make you a gift of the fare."

Her pretty mouth grew firm. "Out of the question. I always pay my own way, Danny."

He slewed slightly in his seat to look at her. "Not even a birthday present?"

"You can send me a card."

"And that's all you want?" He seemed pleased.

"That's all I want. My gran always said you should pay your own way in this world." God alone knew Maisy had paid her way, *scraped* her way sometimes, but she'd kept her integrity intact, which was a damn sight more than could be said for... for her grandfather.

"Your gran sounds like one hell of a nice lady," Danny said, maneuvering the car around a curve with practiced ease.

"She was. She was very special." It still hurt, using the past tense when she talked about Maisy, and the familiar burning sensation started behind her eyes. She blinked hard. If she started bawling, she had a feeling she wouldn't be able to stop.

"Well," he said, "there's nothing else for it. If Muhammad won't go to the mountain, the mountain must come to Muhammad." He took his eyes briefly off the road to glance at her. "I'll have to come to England."

"Oh!"

Of course, when you had money things were simple. All you needed was money for a ticket, and separation became just a word.

"That's what I like," he said. "An enthusiastic response."

"I hadn't thought..." She hadn't thought about *anything*. "It might be nice...."

"I'm overwhelmed by your reaction," he said dryly, "but I guess it'll have to do for now."

She gave him a sidelong glance. The harsh planes of his face were accentuated by the light from the dash, exaggerating the hawklike nose, the sensual curve of his lips.... She looked away. It was bad enough being his first cousin without compounding it with feelings of lust.

"Will you drive back to Halifax with me tomorrow?" he asked, increasing speed now that they were on a straight stretch of road.

"I can't," she said. "I've rented a car." As if that were any reason to refuse. The real reason was sheer panic. Panic at her own emotions.

"But you drop the car off in St. John's, don't you?" he queried.

"Well, yes...."

"So, drop it off and then come on the ferry with me. Once we dock in Cape Breton it's a lovely drive along the Cabot Trail."

She looked at the road ahead as if fascinated by the beam of the headlights. To drive on the celebrated Cabot Trail with Danny would be wonderful, but she didn't dare risk it. Not now that she'd finally faced the true bond between them. The bond of blood.

"I have a plane ticket," she said flatly.

He dismissed this. "That's no problem. You can get a refund. My secretary will do it for you when we get to Halifax."

"I'm perfectly capable of getting my own refund, thank you," she said tartly. "That is, if I wanted one, which I don't. I intend to fly."

"But why, when—"

"Because I *want* to," she nearly shouted.

"Don't be so dumb."

"And don't *you* be so bloody domineering." It was a relief to replace panic with anger, and she fanned the flames—hard. "Patronizing me—"

"Selby, for God's sake!"

"—calling me names just because I don't automatically do what you want...."

"I didn't call you names." He slowed the car to a crawl.

"Oh, yes, you did! You said I was dumb."

"Well, so you are. The Cabot Trail is one of the most beautiful drives in Canada."

"For heaven's sake, stop going on about it!" fumed Selby. There seemed to be a refuge in anger, and so she carried on heedlessly down that path. "Hasn't it occurred to you that I might want to be alone for a bit, that I might not want your marvelous company all the time—"

She stopped abruptly, because the next logical thing to say was, "I fancy you like mad, as a matter of fact, but you're my first cousin, and it's not a very good idea," but she couldn't bring herself to say it.

"Fine," Danny said quietly. "Why didn't you say so in the first place?" His face looked carved in stone.

"You never give a person a chance to say anything," she muttered, and they both lapsed into silence.

It only took a few minutes to get to Savage Harbour after this exchange, but it felt like hours. Selby, all her false anger evaporated, felt sick at heart, but she could do nothing to ease the tension, for the silence between them was like a lead blanket, too heavy for her to lift.

He drew up in front of the store, switched off the engine, and they both sat, looking out into the darkness. Finally he said, "I plan on getting an early start, so I guess I won't be seeing you in the morning."

"Oh." She couldn't bring herself to say goodbye, either; in any case, there seemed to be a piece of Newfoundland granite lodged in her throat.

He said it for her. "Goodbye, Selby. Maybe we'll meet again in Halifax."

She nodded, forcing herself to look at him, hoping those dark eyes would gaze warmly back at her, melting the ice that was forming over her heart, because unwise though that might be, she didn't think she could take much more of this coldness.

He stared doggedly out at the night. "Then again, maybe not." Abruptly he got out of the car and came around to open the door for her.

"Well . . . goodbye," she said at last, willing him to kiss her. Willing him to take her in his arms. To hell with safety, with propriety. All that mattered was to be safe in his protecting arms.

He stood as impassive as a statue, and as cold.

She turned to go, but when he called after her, "Aren't you forgetting something?" she turned back, caution thrown to the winds, her lips parted, already imagining his mouth on hers.

He held out the package Jim had given her. "This is yours."

"Oh, yes." She took it in cold fingers, her heart as heavy as one of Lisa's sculptures. "Good night."

She heard him mutter, "Good*bye,* Selby," as she went into the store.

Up in her room she sat in the dark for a minute, fighting tears. Tear were stupid. She had hardly cried when her grandmother died, so to cry over Danny and the fact that they were too closely related for comfort was nothing but self-pity, and she refused to give in to that.

The parcel was still lying on her lap. She turned on the bedside lamp and tore off the wrapping, and the tears she had fought so bravely flooded her eyes. Her gift from the Merrills was a small framed watercolor of Danny's lighthouse.

She cried silently, bitterly, for a while, then, wiping the tears away with the back of her hand, she got up and started packing. There was no need to pack to-night like someone poised for instant flight—she had decided to wait until Danny had left in the morning before putting in an appearance—but it gave her something to do. It kept the tears that still clogged her throat at bay.

She wrapped Jim's picture in a scarf and put it at the bottom of her suitcase. In a little while, a few years perhaps, she would be able to look at it without a pang, but for the time being she would keep it out of sight.

WHEN SHE AWOKE in the morning, Danny's station wagon was no longer parked by the store.

He'd left before dawn, Lori told her. "Mac saw him when he was going out to check on his gear. The sun not even up."

Beverly pushed oatmeal around in her bowl disconsolately. "He didn't even say goodbye, an' he didn't come *near* the store last night." She glared at Selby.

"He was visitin' friends. You aren't the only person in the world," Lori said sharply.

Beverly complained, "He might have said goodbye to us, just the same."

"Well, he did," her mother told her. "He said goodbye to your Dad an' me before he drove off. You was still snorin'. Now stop makin' mudpies out of your oatmeal. The school bus'll be here before you know it, an' you not even had a bite."

"I'm not hungry," Beverly muttered, but one look from her mother shut her up, and she finished her oatmeal in record time.

"Don't forget to send us a copy of your story when it comes out," Lori reminded Selby. "An' drop us a line once in a while. We get awful bored in winter, an' news from away is welcome."

Selby nodded, although once she'd sent them the article she knew she wouldn't write to them again. Correspondence between herself and Savage Harbour would be like tearing skin off a healing wound. She wondered what Danny would tell these people about her relationship with his family. She couldn't see him explaining the sins of his grandfather....

The school bus arrived, and Beverly, grabbing her satchel, made for the door. Her mother called her back. "You haven't said goodbye to Selby, Bev."

"Goodbye," the girl mumbled, not looking in Selby's direction.

"Goodbye, Beverly. I hope life turns out well for you," said Selby, thinking it was a good deal better for Beverly at the moment than she realized. Her crush on Danny would soon pass. Selby wasn't so sure about her own infatuation.

"I'll be that relieved when our Bev is over hormones," Lori said with a sigh as her daughter left, slamming the door after her. "She don't mean to be rude. It's just she's got this idea about Danny...."

"Yes," said Selby, "I know the feeling."

"She'll get over it soon enough, but it feels like life an' death while it's goin' on."

"Yes," Selby said, "I know."

"Well, I can't stand here chattin' all mornin'," Lori said. "We'll miss you, Selby, but life has to go on."

"I suppose it does." She finished her coffee and settled her bill. It was modest, but Selby knew better than to offend the Pyecrofts by adding a tip. "Well, I'll be on my way," she said, holding out her hand.

Lori ignored the hand and kissed her cheek, instead. "Drive carefully," she said gruffly. "An' next time, for heaven's sake, give us some notice, so we can fix up the room proper." Then she stomped down to the cellar, muttering something about hating goodbyes and if she was going, why didn't she get a move on?

Everything seemed out of sorts this morning, thought Selby, even the weather. As she drove away it started to rain, and her farewell glimpse of the lighthouse was shrouded in mist like a fading memory— although she suspected the memory would never fade completely, but remain in the recesses of her mind long after she'd stopped consciously thinking about Savage Harbour.

The trip back to Halifax was uneventful. Once there Selby booked into a small downtown hotel, unpacked her few clothes, then, taking a deep breath to steady herself, phoned Daniel Forest's house. The sooner she faced him, got it over with and left town, the better.

The housekeeper answered. She remembered Selby. "Did you go to Newfoundland, Miss? Did you see Mr. Danny?"

"Yes, thank you." *And how I wish I hadn't.* "I wondered if... if the family had returned from Europe?"

By her calculations they should have, and the housekeeper confirmed this by telling her that they'd gotten back the previous night. "Did you want to speak to Mrs. Forest?" she asked.

Momentarily flustered, Selby agreed. She'd intended to ask for Danny's grandfather, but on second thought, perhaps it was better to make her appointment through a third party. She didn't trust herself to be polite if she spoke to the elder Daniel directly, and to confront him over the phone was useless. He would just hang up on her and, if she arrived at his house after that, refuse to see her.

After a few moments a woman's voice said, "Mary Forest here. Can I help you?" She sounded breathless, as if she'd hurried from somewhere.

"I hope so," said Selby, introducing herself. "I'm visiting from England—"

Mrs. Forest interrupted. "Oh, I know, dear! You're the girl who's been with Danny at Savage Harbour."

"You...you know?" said Selby, startled. "How?"

Mrs. Forest laughed. "Why, Danny told us, of course."

"*Danny* did?" squeaked Selby.

"Yes. He phoned us a couple of days ago when we were in London, and he said you were with him. We're *dying* to know you."

"I was wondering if I might pay you a visit?" said Selby, thinking they wouldn't be so keen to know her when they found out what she had to say.

Laughter bubbled through the receiver. "My dear! You make it sound so formal. Of course you must visit. We naturally assumed that Danny would be bringing you over as soon as you both got back from Newfoundland."

"Danny's not with me, Mrs. Forest." *And never will be again, more's the pity.*

"Oh, isn't he? How peculiar. Where is he, dear?"

"On the ferry, I suppose."

"*You* didn't come on the ferry, then?"

"No. I took the plane and—"

Mary Forest interrupted again. "But I was sure Danny told me you'd be traveling together. I know I sometimes get things wrong, but I'm sure that's what he said."

He probably had. Presuming, in that high-handed manner of his, that she'd accept his invitation to travel with him without a second thought.

"There was a change of plans," Selby explained quickly before Mrs. Forest had time to start another barrage of questions. "I don't have much time left in Canada, and I simply *must* see you before I go home. At least," she corrected herself, "I must see Danny's grandfather and—"

But Mrs. Forest had started talking before Selby had finished her sentence. "How *sweet* of you, dear! And again so *formal*. But then, the English are, aren't they? Formal, I mean, but so *nice*, once you get to know them. I tell you what—come tomorrow for brunch."

"Oh, I don't think so," said Selby hastily. A meal was not included in her plans for retribution.

"About noon," the implacable Mary Forest went on.

"Mrs. Forest, I just want to drop in for a moment—"

"We should have caught up on our sleep by then, and we'll be a bit more sociable. I should have finished putting the garden back into some sort of order, too. You can't *imagine* the mess the gardeners have made of it without me to bully them. It will take me *months* to bring it—and them—back into shape—"

"Mrs. Forest, I really can't come for brunch," said Selby, desperately trying to stem the flow.

"—so you be here at noon tomorrow," Mary Forest went on, undeterred. "You can't guess how anxious I am to meet you, Selby. We all are. And, Selby,

we're so pleased for Danny. Now I must dash. I can
see that idiot Albert putting my new bulbs in the
wrong place. I *told* him not under the big pine—the
squirrels practically *live* there.'' Before Selby had time
to even say goodbye she had hung up.

She couldn't have asked for a warmer welcome. Far
too warm for the interview Selby planned. What on
earth had Danny told them? Whatever it was, Mary
Forest was in for a shock—and so was Danny's
grandfather. One thing was certain—the Forests' ea-
gerness to take her into the family bosom would
change once they discovered the reason for her visit.
They would probably whisk the eggs Benedict—or
whatever they served for brunch—away from her and
show her the door. But not before she'd had her say.
She'd waited too long to be cheated out of that.

She spent the rest of the day exploring Halifax—
Danny's town, where he lived and worked. Even in her
mood of current tension it enchanted her. She discovered the old brewery, which was now a beautifully re-
stored complex of shops and restaurants, and bought
gifts for the girls in the office. When she climbed Cit-
adel Hill, the sun came out. Gulls mewed and dipped
in the salty breeze, while children played and adults
lounged on the grass-covered fortress, enjoying the last
gasp of summer.

Danny's town. She found she couldn't stop thinking about him, and, irritated by her lack of discipline,
she decided that strenuous exercise was called for, so
she set off for Point Pleasant Park and a hike on one
of its many nature trails.

The hike was long, but her restlessness remained unabated, although she was worn-out by the time she arrived at the seawall.

Sitting eating an ice-cream cone on a bench facing the sea, she watched a large container vessel waiting to dock and discharge its cargo at one of the piers. At one of Danny's container piers, perhaps?

Danny again. He stuck in her mind with the tenacity of one of those limpets he studied, and if she walked her feet off to the ankles, she suspected she would still be unable to shake him loose. He was anchored to her heart the way kelp anchors itself to rock. And that was courting disaster. He was her cousin. Her first cousin, nearly as close in blood as a brother.

At least he wouldn't be around when she finally met ... their grandfather. She'd leave Halifax right after that. Leave tomorrow afternoon. See a bit of the countryside.

Once she'd put the trauma of her meeting with Daniel Forest behind her, she'd make a holiday out of her remaining time in Canada. It would be fun, she insisted hollowly, but her appetite for pistachio-nut ice cream had vanished, and she dumped the rest of the cone into a nearby waste bin.

CHAPTER EIGHT

THE NEXT MORNING started badly.

Her emerald suit was creased, so to take out the wrinkles, she hung it on the shower rail and turned the hot tap on. Then she went back to the bedroom to go through the rest of her wardrobe.

Brunch was normally an informal meal, so she decided to wear her leather boots instead of high-heeled pumps. There were still faint salt stains around the toes, and she rubbed at them vigorously, but they were as enduring as the memory of that first meeting with Danny. Although she buffed until the leather shone like new chestnuts and her arm ached, she couldn't get rid of an uneven white thread of salt. Disgusted, she flung them away and settled for tan loafers.

She returned to the bathroom to find an empty hanger on the shower rail; the shower was on full, and the emerald suit was lying in the tub, a drenched and sodden lump.

Lips set, she picked it up, rolled it in a towel to remove some of the water and rehung it on the hanger, where it dangled shapelessly, like a particularly vivid bunch of seaweed.

She went back to the cupboard and took out a beige linen skirt, pulled a clay-colored sweater over her curls, which this morning had decided to be more unruly than usual, and gazed sourly at herself in the mirror.

Her skirt was very short and tight, her sweater hugged her small, high breasts a little too provocatively, and her mop of riotous curls made her look more like a dizzy sixteen, instead of a serious twenty-four. This was not the impression she'd planned to convey.

She fiddled in her jewelry pouch for Maisy's brooch to pin to the neck of her sweater, for she needed all the emotional support she could muster, but she was clumsy and the brooch dropped from her fingers, the pin catching her on the ankle and putting a run in her last pair of panty hose.

"Damn and blast!" she hissed through gritted teeth. It was Sunday and no stores were open, so she couldn't buy new ones till the next day.

Cursing heartily, she kicked off her loafers and pulled on her boots—salt stains or no salt stains, at least they hid the run. She'd planned to apply lipstick, but the way the morning was shaping up she was likely to smear it all over herself and arrive at the Forest residence looking like a runaway from a circus. So she left her lips unpainted and contented herself with a touch of mascara and a dab of perfume behind her ears.

The morning continued the way it had started. She had difficulty finding a taxi, and it was half-past twelve by the time she arrived at the house on the North West Arm.

She was too agitated about being late, about having a run in her hose and wearing a skirt that needed ironing to notice there were a lot of cars in the driveway.

Before ringing the bell, she checked the documents in her purse, just to make sure she hadn't forgotten them in the general confusion: her mother's birth certificate, the photograph of Maisy and Selby's mother, Maisy's death certificate. She swallowed hard, her heart pounding.

She'd imagined that when the moment of confrontation arrived, she would be very aware of her grandmother's presence, as if Maisy were standing in the shadows encouraging her, but Maisy had never seemed so far away as she did at this moment, and Selby had never felt so alone.

She rang the bell and touched the pin at her neck for courage, pricking her finger. A bead of blood welled out of the wound. "Damn and blast!" said Selby for the umpteenth time this morning, hoping this wasn't a bad omen. Sucking at her finger, she rang the bell again.

Nothing happened. There was a fine dew of perspiration on her upper lip, although the breeze that blew in off the sea was cool. She rang a third time, a long, insistent peal. Finally the housekeeper she'd met before opened the door.

"Sorry, miss, I was in the kitchen. There's such a racket going on I didn't hear you." She smiled warmly, and now Selby became aware of a muted roar of voices coming from the hidden regions of the house.

"Oh," she croaked, her throat suddenly lined with sandpaper, "it sounds like a party."

"It's all right, miss," the woman reassured her. "They're expecting you."

"But I really only wanted to see Daniel Forest. The elder Daniel Forest, that is," Selby said.

"Mr. and Mrs. Forest are both expecting you," the housekeeper said blandly, leading the way down the hall. Selby, mute and powerless, followed, the heels of her boots sinking into the deep-pile of the carpeting, the dowager scent of roses from numerous vases filling her nostrils.

"Here we are!" said the housekeeper, flinging wide double doors and motioning Selby to step inside. "Mrs. Forest's over there. Now, please excuse me. I've got cheese straws in the oven."

It was a very large room with about sixty people milling about in it. A middle-aged woman detached herself from a group by the fireplace and came toward her.

"Selby?" She was a handsome, untidy-looking woman, gray hair falling out of a knot on top of her head, amber beads slung carelessly around her neck. "My dear! I'm Mary Forest, Danny's mother. How lovely to meet you at last."

She took Selby's arm and pulled her into the room. She wore a number of beautiful rings, but her hands were work stained, the nails cut short and unpolished. "I'm sorry about this zoo. It sort of grew like Topsy, but they should all leave in a couple of hours, and then we can have a nice chat."

Selby found her voice. "Mrs. Forest, I really came to see—"

"I want to hear all about you," interrupted Danny's mother. "Danny told us you were a journalist. Is that right?"

"Yes, but—" she tried again "—Mrs. Forest, I really can't stay."

Mary Forest smiled at her. Her smile was disconcertingly like her son's, though the resemblance ended there. She was tall, but her eyes were bright blue, and her face had none of Danny's angularity. "Don't be shy, my dear."

"I'm not shy—"

"Of course you're not. But all these people…" She looked at the throng dubiously. "I don't know half of them. Lawyer friends of Henry's, I suppose. Did Danny tell you his father is a lawyer?"

"Yes. I must talk—"

"Well, I suppose it's nice to have a lawyer in the family," she went on. "Although it's my opinion that being a lawyer tends to make one too suspicious, though I grant you he was right about that other business. I mean, she not only took me in, she took in Dad, as well. Of course, she was pretty," she added thoughtfully. Then, patting Selby's hand, she said, "But not in the nice, natural way you are, dear, but that's in the past, isn't it?"

"Mrs. Forest," said Selby in an attempt to stop this flow, "I don't think you understand—"

She might as well have tried to stop molten lava. "Oh, my dear! You haven't got a drink!" cried her hostess. "I'm a terrible hostess. I can't *imagine* what

you must think of me. Dad's always complaining that
I'm hopeless, but I always tell him you can't make a
hollyhock out of a sweet pea." She laughed gaily.
"*That* generally shuts him up, and shutting up Henry's father takes some doing, believe me. Here we are!
You'll have a glass of mimosa, won't you? I wanted to
serve fuzzy navels, but Henry drew the line."

Gratefully Selby accepted a glass of champagne and
orange juice. Five minutes in Mary Forest's company
had generated the need for strong drink. "What is a
fuzzy navel?" she asked groggily.

"Orange juice, peach schnapps and champagne,"
Mary Forest told her. "Simply delicious, *I* think, but
Henry doesn't agree." A sudden thought struck her.
"Oh! You haven't met Henry yet, have you?"

"I haven't met *anyone* yet," Selby replied desperately, "but I've come to see—"

"Well, I mustn't monopolize you, my dear." She
called out to a tall, thin man who was standing with a
group on the grass. "Henry, come and meet Selby.
You know, Danny's new friend, Selby. Come along.
You can talk business later."

Selby, wondering if Danny's father was as over-
powering as his mother, prepared herself for another
verbal onslaught. She needn't have worried. Henry
Forest came up to them, nodded tersely, but didn't
utter a word.

Mary Forest rattled on. "This is my husband,
Henry. He's been dying to meet you, as well, Selby.
You mustn't mind if he seems reserved. It's his way."

And who could blame him? thought Selby. It was a
miracle his vocal cords hadn't atrophied. She took a

good look at Danny's father and felt a little jolt of recognition.

He had a shock of black hair like his son, but his was touched with gray, and he had the same craggy features and wide sensual mouth, and although his eyes were not as dark as Danny's, nor his shoulders as broad, the resemblance was unmistakable.

"Very nice to meet you, Selby," he said, but there was a wariness in his welcome, and Selby sensed she was being carefully assessed.

"Henry, those idiots are going down to the dahlias!" cried his wife. "I must stop them. They'll trample them to bits. Will you take care of Selby? Introduce her to people?" She smiled at Selby vaguely. "Later on, when this mob's cleared off, we can have a nice cozy chat."

"I really can't..." started Selby, but Mary Forest was already making her way down the lawn.

"You mustn't mind my wife," said her husband. "She never listens. We're used to it, but it can be a bit bewildering to outsiders."

Selby had the distinct impression that he used the term "outsiders" deliberately. But at least he seemed willing to give her a chance to talk.

"I'm a bit embarrassed," she said, "about being invited to this party. I came to Canada to meet your father. That's what I've been trying to explain to Mrs. Forest."

She was trying to figure out the relationship between herself and Henry Forest. If he was her cousin's father, he must be her...her uncle. Not that he was looking particularly avuncular at the moment.

"Danny said something about your trying to contact my father," he said. "Your grandmother knew him, it seems?"

"Yes. They met during the war, in England." She hoped she sounded offhand. "They became . . . very good friends."

Not entirely untrue. It just depended on your interpretation of "good friends."

"Strange. I don't remember Dad mentioning anything about having a woman friend over there."

"It was a long time ago," she said. "Nineteen forty-two, to be exact."

It was hardly the sort of thing he *would* discuss with his children, was it?

"Mmm." Henry Forest held out a dish of nuts.

"No, thank you." She put her half-finished drink down on one of the tables. "If I could see your father alone for a few minutes, I'm sure he'd remember Maisy Tredwell." *And if he doesn't, I fully intend to jog his memory.*

Henry Forest chewed a macadamia nut thoughtfully. "I'm afraid that's not possible," he said.

The guarded look was still there, and Selby was beginning to think he did know about Maisy, and that he intended to protect his father from scandal at all costs. She lifted her chin combatively. "Why is that?"

"He's still in England," said Henry. "On a walking tour of the Lake District with an old friend."

"Oh, come on!" she said derisively. "At his age?"

He raised his eyebrows, looking very much like Danny when he was irritated. "My father is a very fit seventy-eight."

"I just meant...all those hills...so strenuous...." she amended weakly, picking up her champagne cocktail again and downing it. There was no
point making an enemy of this man.

"He likes a challenge—we all do," Henry informed her coldly. "Now, let me introduce you to
some of our younger guests. They'll be more fun for
you than us old fogies."

It was very deftly executed, and before she'd had a
chance to say it was time she was going, she had been
handed a plate of food and was being guided toward
a table by a young man.

He introduced himself and started making small
talk. Selby didn't listen. She couldn't; she was in too
much of a quandary. Her brilliant plan was a total
flop. Danny's grandfather still eluded her, his father
was suspicious, Mary Forest seemed to think Selby
was romantically involved with her son, and she was
no nearer claiming retribution for Maisy than she'd
been when she set out on her journey.

She pushed her plate aside. "I'm afraid I have to go
now," she told the young man. "It's been nice meeting you."

"But you haven't touched your food," he said.
"Are you feeling ill?"

She stood up. "No, but I have to go."

She didn't want to stay here any longer, living a lie,
making everything worse. She would go back to her
hotel, appraise her options—if she had any—and lick
her wounds in private.

The young man stood, too. "If you hang on for a bit," he said, "I'll be happy to drive you. My car's here."

"It's kind of you, but no, thank you."

"It's no trouble," he insisted. "I was thinking of leaving myself."

This was patently untrue, but Selby had stopped listening to what he was saying. She was staring past him at the tall, dark figure of a man talking to Mary Forest.

The woman turned, saw Selby looking at them and waved. "He's arrived early!" she cried happily. "Isn't that great?"

"Great!" muttered Selby weakly, sitting down again.

Danny came over to her. "Selby! What a nice surprise." He nodded curtly to the young man. "Hello, Kevin. Still climbing the corporate ladder?"

"I thought you were still in New Brunswick," Kevin muttered.

"Newfoundland." Danny drew up a chair and sat down at their table.

"Do join us," Kevin said sourly. He turned to Selby. "Are you staying now?"

"Of course she's staying." Danny smiled. Selby felt her heart give a little twinge, and she wondered if that was what it felt like when it started to break.

"I really should be going," she mumbled.

"No, you shouldn't," Danny said firmly. "Believe me, you should not."

"I was about to drive her home," Kevin said, "but now that you've turned up..."

"That's right," Danny declared firmly. "I'll look after her now."

"I don't need anyone to look after me!" snapped Selby. "I'm quite capable of getting back to the hotel by myself."

"But not just yet," said Danny. "We have to talk, Selby."

Kevin got to his feet. "I guess I'm in the way."

"No," said Selby.

"Yes," said Danny.

Kevin shrugged. "If you change your mind about the lift," he said to Selby, "let me know."

Danny waited until Kevin had gone before saying, "I don't flatter myself that you came here to find me."

"I came because I wanted to see your grandfather."

"Of course. Well—" he took a slice of smoked salmon from her plate "—you're out of luck. He's still in England."

"I know. Your father told me."

"Here!" He put the salmon on a slice of brown bread and offered it to her.

She shook her head. "No, thank you."

"You should eat more," he told her, putting it on her side plate. "You've got to keep up your strength for pursuing Granddad."

"I'm not pursuing him," she objected.

He took a grape and ate it absentmindedly. "I don't know what else you'd call it. Chasing off to Canada on a whim—"

"It wasn't a whim," she protested, although she knew that was exactly what Maisy would have called it.

"—rushing all over the country to find him—"

"And finding the wrong man," she broke in accusingly.

He looked at her for a moment, a laser glance. "You didn't find the wrong man, Selby, and you know it."

She flushed scarlet. She hardly ever blushed, but around Danny she seemed to blush as readily as a Victorian heroine. "I know nothing of the kind. And while we're on the subject, what did you tell your parents about me? About us? Your father keeps looking at me as if I'm about to make off with the family silver, and your mother seems to think we're about to elope."

"Ah, well, Dad's a lawyer. He comes by his caution naturally."

"That doesn't explain your mother."

"*Nothing* explains my mother," he told her cheerfully.

She looked at him sternly, her gray eyes framed by long, curling lashes. "It's not good enough, Danny. You must have said *something*. She was carrying on as if we were about to—" she hesitated a moment "—become engaged."

"All I said was that I'd met a charming, nutty girl, and that I'd fallen in love with her," he said calmly.

She was assailed by savage joy, which was instantly replaced by panic. "You can't be. You don't know me."

"Not very well, but I plan to get to know you better. And yes, I can."

All kinds of emotions were struggling inside her, and now the principal one was dismay. Why, oh, why did life have to be so difficult? Why did they have to share the same grandparent?

"It's not possible," she said. "Believe me, it's not possible."

He looked at her through narrowed eyes. "I don't believe you."

"Well, you'd better," she said, her nerves jangling. "I don't mean to be rude, but you don't even turn me on."

He got up from his chair with his characteristic animal grace. "In that case you won't object to a little experiment," he said, taking her firmly by the arm and pulling her up, too.

"Let me go!" she protested as he marched her briskly toward the door.

He said tightly, "Shut up, sweetheart. I guarantee this isn't going to hurt."

By now they were in the hall, and he pulled her along after him till they reached a room near the front of the house. He opened the door and drew her inside. It was a dim, book-lined room. She had a fleeting impression of leather armchairs, Turkish rugs, the smell of furniture polish.

"Now," said Danny, putting both arms around her, "let's see if I'm the wrong man."

She had no time to prepare herself, to compel herself not to respond or to feel resentment that he was taking advantage of her. She had no time for anything except the realization that being in his arms was the most natural thing in the world.

His arms felt strong and comforting. Arousing, too, and she felt her body starting to tremble. He began to caress her, kissing the nape of her neck, stroking her small, high breasts, and she heard herself moan with longing.

"Sweetheart, sweet Selby," he muttered, claiming her lips again when she arched against him, and all she could think of was the taste of him, the feel of him pressed hard against her, the need that swept over her like Atlantic breakers.

He released her at last and held her away from him, searching her face with an intensity that frightened her. "Do you still insist I'm the wrong man?" he asked, his breathing as unsteady as hers.

Her eyes grew evasive as reality came crashing back. "You're crazy. We've only known each other a few days."

"Time has nothing to do with it," he answered harshly. "You can't deny the feeling between us."

"I'm sure you've felt lust before," she said, trying to sound flippant and failing dismally.

For a moment he looked so grim she flinched inwardly, but all he said was, "Don't cheapen yourself, Selby. And don't cheapen me."

"No, really, Danny—" she took a step away from him on legs that felt like strands of cooked spaghetti "—we mustn't get carried away."

"Stop talking like some little tart I picked up on the waterfront," he said harshly. "You know as well as I do that what's between us is special. Why won't you admit it?''

If only she could have said, ''Because if I admit it, I'm lost. . . .'' But she couldn't say that, so instead she shrilled, ''Why? Because I refuse to become another of your conquests, that's why.''

''Conquests! What the hell are you talking about?''

Again she took refuge in anger, twisting the emotions he had unleashed into something hard and ugly.

''I recognize your sort,'' she blundered on thoughtlessly. ''Lori said you've always had plenty of women around, and now you want to add me to the list. Well, nothing doing, chum. I'm not interested in a tumble with someone I met five days ago, so you can just forget it.''

He said, his voice as rough as the bark of a tree, ''You haven't understood a thing I've been telling you, have you? I don't happen to be interested in a tumble—to use your repellent term—either.''

''You could have fooled me there,'' she interrupted angrily.

''And I wasn't trying to rush you into my bed, although I do admit I want you. But you know that. You'd have to be even nuttier than you are not to know that.''

''And what Danny wants Danny gets. Is that the drill?''

''For God's sake, stop talking like a recruit in an army platoon.'' The muscle in his cheek was twitching, a sure sign of controlled fury. ''As I recall, you weren't exactly fighting me off.''

"Well, you're bigger than I am," she mumbled.

"I hoped that my...experiment would prove that the attraction between us isn't all on one side. But apparently you refuse to admit it."

Her counterfeit anger drained away, leaving her spent. Miserable. "Anything between us...it just isn't possible, Danny," she insisted.

"You *are* married, then?" His dark eyes seemed to bore holes into her.

"No."

"But there's someone else?"

To lie would have made things so much easier. To have said that she was already committed. But she couldn't do it. There were too many half-truths between them already.

She took a ragged breath. "There's no one else."

"Then *why?*" He raked his fingers through his hair. "For the sweet Lord's sake, why?"

She nearly said, "Because what I want from you, my darling, is a lifelong commitment. A marriage—with children. But we are first cousins, and that kind of risk isn't possible, and I won't—I can't—settle for less."

Besides, if she told him and he didn't care, if he said he wanted her anyway, would she still have the strength to refuse him? She loved him so much. Safer to continue keeping the knowledge of their relationship a secret and make him believe she despised him—even if it felt like tearing the heart out of her body.

"Stop trying to rush me off my feet, Danny," she said wildly. "It just confuses me and...and..."

He looked at her, his expression wary. "And?"

She drew a faltering breath. "It's just not possible. Take my word for it."

"I'm afraid I can't take your word, Selby," he said evenly. "I might be mad about you, but I'm not quite a fool—not anymore."

"There's no point in all this," she said, making for the door.

He caught her arm. "What's really going on, Selby? Why did you come to Canada in the first place?"

"I told you," she said.

"To meet a man your grandmother knew forty years ago?"

She couldn't speak, her mouth was as dry as sand, so she did the next best thing and nodded wordlessly.

"I don't believe you, my angel," he said with a calm that scared the wits out of her. "You're not being honest. What's really going on?"

"I promised Gran..." she croaked, knowing full well now that the only person she had promised was herself.

"To look up this old friend of hers?"

She was sinking into quicksand. Helpless against his interrogation. "What is this? The Inquisition?"

"You'd go to all this trouble just to look up an acquaintance of your grandmother's?"

"She was *dying*." Suddenly her voice cracked, tears were imminent.

"But this has nothing to do with *us*," he insisted, "and it doesn't explain why you want me but then you fight me off." She went to speak but he held up his hand. "No. Don't say again that you're not attracted to me, because we both know that's not true."

"Physical attraction isn't enough for me," she said, grasping at straws.

"And you believe that's all there is between us?"

"Yes," she lied.

"I don't buy that, Selby. What's wrong?"

"Affairs, even fleeting ones, take time," she drawled, hoping she sounded world-weary. "I simply don't have the energy."

"Who says it has to be fleeting?"

"It couldn't be anything else, given the circumstances." She spoke so softly he had to bend to hear her.

"What circumstances, sweetheart?"

His sympathy terrified her more than harsh words ever could, and in self-defense she railed at him. "For pity's sake, you're not God's gift, you know. Hasn't it occurred to you that I simply want to get away from you?"

His face became shuttered again. An impenetrable mask. He opened the door. "On your way, then."

She stumbled out and heard him click the door shut before she had a chance to realize just what she had done.

CHAPTER NINE

SHE WALKED BRISKLY down the front path. Her eyes were so full of tears that rose beds and lawns wavered and shimmered, their colors swimming together like a kaleidoscope.

When she reached the gate, she was overtaken by a car. Kevin wound down the window and asked, "Can you use that lift?"

Since she had no idea how she was to get back to town, she didn't hesitate. Kevin's appearance was a gift from the gods. "That would be great. Thanks."

The car was a low-slung sporty job, gleaming with chrome and bristling with gadgets. Selby slid into the passenger seat, her tight skirt riding uncomfortably high.

"Nice gams!" Kevin remarked. "You a dancer?"

She wasn't too keen on the look he gave her, but since she'd only just climbed in, she could hardly climb out again.

"Nothing so exotic."

She tugged at her skirt, which seemed to be anchored somewhere around her waist. If she'd thought about it, she could have phoned for a cab, but all she'd wanted to do was get away from the house, away from Danny, and there hadn't been time to think about anything. She'd have to write a note to her host and hostess thanking them for their hospitality, and that would be her last contact with the Forests. That would be the *end*.

When they reached the highway Kevin pressed his foot hard on the accelerator. The car sprang forward with a roar. "What do *you* do for a living?" she asked. "Drive racing cars?"

"Wish I did," he said, "but I'm a corporate lawyer with Henry's firm."

"That must be interesting," she said. She found corporate law about as interesting as soybeans, but if she was getting a lift, the least she could do was make an effort to be sociable.

When they were on the road, Kevin thrust a tape into the deck and a blast of rock music nearly burst her eardrums. She must have winced, for he lowered the volume. "Too loud for you?"

"A bit. My ears are out of practice."

"I'm not surprised, if you've been hanging out with Danny," said Kevin. "He goes in for that classical crap, if I remember."

"I happen to like that classical crap," Selby snapped, remembering with a pang the Vivaldi tapes Danny had played on their drives in Newfoundland.

"Ah, well. To each his own." He pushed the eject button. "There are some musicals in there some-where." He nodded to a black plastic file filled with tapes. "Or don't you like musicals, either?"

"I love musicals. But I don't feel like any music right now." Music was dangerous. It released all kinds of emotions she wasn't capable of dealing with. "I've got a ... a bit of a headache."

"Too much vino? Best thing for a hangover is the hair of the dog. How about coming back to my place for a drink?"

Oh, lor! she thought. He doesn't waste any time. It must be the short skirt. "No, thank you. It's air I want, not alcohol."

"Then let's go to Peggy's Cove. Lots of air there."

"I should go back to my hotel," she told him. "Pack ... and organize myself for the rest of my holiday." *Run away* was what she meant.

Kevin dismissed this. "You can't come to Nova Scotia and not see Peggy's Cove. It's against the law."

So they went to Peggy's Cove and tramped over a moonscape of rocks worn smooth by the ceaseless motion of the sea. Hunched against a biting wind, Selby faced the fact that she'd never felt so miserable in her life, and it didn't seem to do any good telling herself that all that had happened was a row with a man she hardly knew. She still felt as if her soul had been torn out of her.

"... and I sat up all night in that unheated airport, but I'd closed the deal *and* saved the firm megabucks, so it was worth it," said Kevin, finishing some rambling story that Selby hadn't bothered listening to.

"Wonderful," she said through chattering teeth.

Kevin looked at her. "Hey! You're cold."

"I'll be fine." *When I've chipped the ice off my heart.*

"Let's have coffee. There's a restaurant at the point."

From inside the warm restaurant, Peggy's Cove looked much more cheerful. Today, in spite of the wind, the sea was relatively calm. It would be great in a gale, when the sea was churned into tumbling breakers that crashed on the rocks, sending spray as high as a cathedral ceiling. People came in droves to watch, forgetting that such wild beauty was also perilous. Shipwrecks with all hands lost were not unknown at Peggy's Cove. Maybe that was why, in spite of its beauty, she found it a melancholy place.

She clasped her hands around her mug of steaming coffee, feeling the life coming back into her fingers. Or could it be that the melancholy had taken root inside her when she had walked away from Danny and heard him close the door after her? *That* had felt like the end of her life. She could hear it still, that sad little sound. *Click.* You're dead. *Click.*

"How do you know the Forests?" asked Kevin. "I've never seen you at any of their parties before."

"I'm visiting from the U.K.," she explained. "There's a... family connection."

"You're related, are you?"

"Distantly." Would Kevin be surprised if she said, "Actually, Danny's my first cousin"?

"Funny. Danny never mentioned any relatives in England."

"It's a very distant connection," she said. "Have you known the family a long time?" She didn't want to talk about Danny or his family, but since she seemed incapable of thinking about anything else, she might as well rub salt in the wound.

"All my life. Danny and I were at school together. Not in the same class, of course—he's older than I am—but my folks know his folks, and when we were kids we saw a lot of each other."

"So you must know his grandfather?" Not that she was really interested anymore, but she might as well find out all she could.

"Not very well. I've met him, of course. Crusty old geezer. Danny's a lot like him."

She said, "Danny's not crusty," although it wasn't a bad description.

"I guess you can't be crusty when you're young," he agreed, "but Danny's sure as hell hard to get along with sometimes."

He was that, but a sort of illogical loyalty made her say, "I found him delightful."

Kevin stirred sugar into his coffee moodily. "All women do."

"He's popular with women, isn't he?" asked Selby, bent on suffering.

"They seem to think he's a cross between Sir Galahad and Superman. He ought to ride a white horse."

"Make up your mind," she snapped. "You just finished saying he was crusty."

Kevin drained his coffee cup. "Are you in love with him, too?"

That "too" got her on the raw. "Don't be stupid. I hardly know the man."

'Don't blow a gasket, I was only asking. Anyway, I guess he's still carrying a torch for Beth Lorimer, so you didn't get to experience his charm."

Beth Lorimer. She'd forgotten about her. Was Danny still in love with her? Maybe that explained his keenness to make love to Selby—to use her as a kind of poultice for his broken heart, a kind of romantic Band-Aid. The idea curdled, like vinegar in milk.

She asked Kevin, "What was she like? Beth?"

"Real looker. Legs up to her waist."

"Never mind about her legs. What was she like as a person?"

"Loads of fun," said Kevin. "Not that I knew her that well. I mean, I didn't fly in her league. Couldn't afford to. She's got expensive tastes, has Beth."

Well, Danny could afford her. None of the Forests were exactly financially strapped.

"I guess it's nice to be rich," she said bitterly, and thought how insincere that was, because it wasn't Danny's money that had come between then. The way he behaved, you'd never guess he was wealthy.

"You can say that again," said Kevin, looking at his watch. "Cripes! I've got to get going. My parents are expecting me, and I'm going to be late. This has been real nice, Selby. Sorry I can't take you out this evening."

"I didn't expect you to," she said.

"Sure you did," he said complacently. "Maybe tomorrow?" She muttered something about maybe moving on tomorrow, and he said, "I'll call you at the hotel. If you're still around, we could grab a bite."

She smiled vaguely. If he did phone, it was simple enough not to return his call, for although company would have been nice, she wasn't entirely sure she liked him enough to spend more time with him.

She spent the rest of the evening washing under-
wear and watching TV, only going out to pick up some
Indonesian take-out food to eat in her room. To avoid
thinking, she had to stay busy, and so she scrubbed
until her knuckles were raw, did her nails and plucked
her eyebrows. After her sketchy meal, she watched an
old Alec Guinness movie and kidded herself that she
was having a nice, relaxed evening. If she felt unset-
tled, it was only because the past few days had been
filled with activity. But brushing her teeth in the hotel
bathroom before going to bed, she had a sudden vivid
recollection of Danny's Spartan little bathroom in the
lighthouse, and she felt such longing for him that the
color faded from her face. Her eyes filled with tears,
which she blinked away angrily, telling herself she was
only crying because she'd made her face look lop-
sided by plucking too many hairs out of her right eyebrow.

The following morning she fully intended to go to
the airport and take a flight somewhere, get out of
Halifax, away from the Forest family environs, but
when she was came down to the hotel lobby, a name
on one of the tours the hotel advertised caught her eye.

Uniacke House. That was the place her plane companion had mentioned. Selby scanned the flier. The
white house with its impressive pillared portico looked
attractive, and it was situated in the country. She
hadn't seen anything of the Nova Scotia countryside,
so after a hurried breakfast, she bought a ticket and
climbed aboard the bus. It was too nice a day to leave
Halifax yet.

Uniacke House wasn't very far from town, but it was a pleasant drive. The sun was as bright and warm as summer, and the thickly wooded hills blazed with the bright colors of the Canadian autumn. Selby gazed unseeingly at the panorama and wondered how long she was going to feel like this. Ever since that quarrel, she'd had an impression of being separated from the real world by an invisible sheet of glass. It had never happened to her before and she didn't like it.

They arrived at Uniacke House, and she plodded dutifully through rooms furnished with elegant mahogany furniture, uninterested in quaint wood stoves set in marble hearths, or exquisite patchwork quilts, faded by time like pressed flowers in an old book.

When their guide released them for an hour of free time, Selby went off by herself, unable to take any more of the cheerful, camera-laden crowd.

The gardens sloped gently down to a small steel-dark lake, whose surface glittered like diamonds. Selby followed the path that skirted it, drawing comfort from the soft lapping of water against rock, the swoop of birds in the brilliant sky.

She reached the opposite shore and sat on a bench beneath a paper birch. From here she had a splendid view of the house, and she did her best to make herself admire it while she nibbled at a chocolate bar, which was lunch.

The yellow leaves above her trembled like gold sequins in the sun, and on the lake a pair of ducks floated like toys in a bathtub. Faint sounds of laughter drifted across the water. It was so peaceful, so lovely, and yet...

She carefully wrapped up the chocolate bar and put it back in her purse. She couldn't go on mooning like this over some trivial quarrel. It was ridiculous. She was behaving as if she was hopelessly in love.

A sort of sonic boom went off in her brain and the glass sheet protecting her from pain and reality shattered.

"Oh, no!" she whispered, stricken.

Oh, yes! her heart whispered back. She'd done it again! Leapt without looking. Leapt headlong into love. Because, of course, she was in love with Danny. Utterly, hopelessly, irrevocably in love.

She had been in love with him from the first day, but she had willfully refused to acknowledge the emotion that had grown as steadily, and clung as tenaciously to her being, as any seaweed Danny collected.

That was why she was so reluctant to leave Halifax. It had nothing to do with sight-seeing; she simply couldn't bear to cut the last tie. To lose an opportunity, no matter how remote, of a chance meeting.

She sat, elbows on her knees, her chin in her hands. Like grandmother, like granddaughter! Maisy would have understood her pain. She'd fallen in love at first sight, too, and lived to regret it. But there the comparison ended, for it was Selby who was doing the rejecting, Selby who was running away.

Why, oh, why had Maisy fallen in love with that particular man? There had been plenty of Canadian soldiers in England in 1942. Why couldn't Maisy have fallen in love with someone else? This time Selby didn't blink her tears away but let them creep slowly down her cheeks.

After a while she noticed people collecting at the entrance of Uniacke House. The bus was getting ready to leave. She dried her eyes and started hurrying along the sun-dappled path. On the journey back she'd sort herself out and decide how best to deal with her unhappiness, before it engulfed her forever.

The important thing was to find a way to fall *out* of love as quickly as possible, and she wasn't going to be able to do that by languishing alone all the time. She had to fill her life with company, preferably male, and then the memory of Danny would fade like the quilts at Uniacke House.

That was why she returned Kevin's call when she got back to the hotel.

He took her to one of Halifax's more expensive restaurants, insisting that they drive there even though it was within walking distance.

"We'll need the car after dinner," he said. "It's a long way to my place."

She gave him a sharp look. "I'm not planning on visiting you after dinner."

He swung into the restaurant's parking lot with a squeal of tires. "We can talk about it later."

"We can talk about it now," she replied firmly. "After dinner I want to go home."

He shrugged. "Sure. Relax, Selby, and let's just have a few laughs. Okay?"

"Okay," she said, although laughing was the last thing she felt like doing. There was something too shiny, too self-satisfied about him. She was already sorry she'd agreed to dine with him. She hadn't thought. As usual she'd acted on impulse.

Inside the restaurant he made a fuss because they couldn't get a table by the window, and she shrank with embarrassment when he attempted to bully the maître d' and merely succeeded in arousing the man's contempt.

"This is fine, Kevin," she told him, when they'd been ushered to a table in the center of the room. "Besides, it's such a lovely room it doesn't really matter where we sit."

He pouted unattractively. "*I* like to sit where I can see the sea."

"Well, if the food's as good as you say it is, we'll be too busy eating to pay much attention to the scenery." She sounded as sprightly as a maiden aunt.

"Just the same," he muttered, "I like to get value for my money."

"You can see the sea from here," she replied shortly, wondering if going out with just anybody to help erase the memory of Danny was such a bright idea, after all.

While he went into a huddle with the wine waiter, she looked around the room. The tables that Kevin lusted after were placed against floor-to-ceiling windows, surrounded by pots of chrysanthemums banked against screens that had been discreetly placed to give an air of privacy from the other diners. But one guest was too tall to remain completely hidden, and Selby's hand froze in the act of taking a roll as she saw Danny's dark profile silhouetted against a stand of bronze mums.

"White wine all right with you?"

She forced herself to look back at Kevin. "Wh-what?"

"White wine? Is that okay?"

"Yes. Lovely. Thank you."

What was Danny doing here, of all places? She stole another look at him. He was not alone, but she couldn't make out the other figure behind the screen of plants.

"They're famous for seafood here," Kevin informed her as the waiter thrust a menu into her hands, "so I guess white wine's the thing."

"Yes." She looked down at the menu, not seeing the print.

"I always have the turbot à la meunière," said Kevin. "It's a speciality."

"Yes . . . Well, then, that's what I'll have."

Should she tell Kevin that Danny was here? Better not chance it in case he wanted to go over and chat. The last thing Selby needed was to socialize with Danny. Assuming, of course, that Danny would even acknowledge her after the way they'd parted.

She became aware of Kevin raising his glass. "Here's to having a good time." His eyes seemed to slide over her like oil. "I like your outfit. Sexy."

She'd put on her favorite dress. A two-piece of fuchsia wool challis, cut low in the neck, the skirt falling in graceful folds to midcalf.

Kevin was eyeing her the way a hungry man eyes a steak. "*Very* sexy indeed."

She took a sip from her glass. "Nice wine," she said, although she was feeling so rattled she wouldn't have known if she'd been drinking vinegar.

"Nothing but the best, that's my style," said Kevin. "That's my style in women, too."

For the life of her she couldn't think of a thing to say, so she went on smiling, feeling as if her lips had been stuck in place with glue.

"I need this," said Kevin, draining his glass and helping himself to another. "Been a rough day."

"Really? Anything specific?" As she hoped, he leapt at this conversational gambit and proceeded to go into detail about a particularly difficult case, while Selby's eyes, as if drawn by a magnet, went back to the table by the window.

Danny was leaning forward now in earnest conversation. He looked remarkably elegant, very different from the Danny of Savage Harbour. His jet black hair was seal-sleek, the collar and cuffs of his white shirt dazzling against his dark skin. He passed the salt to his companion and Selby caught a gleam of gold cuff links; the hand that stretched out to receive the salt shaker from him was feminine, and Selby's heart sank another inch.

At that moment he turned to speak to a waiter and caught sight of Selby staring at him. Their eyes locked. Then he looked at Kevin. She turned bright red, but she couldn't look away. She simply couldn't. Danny looked back at her, tilted his head in mocking acknowledgment and returned to deal with the waiter.

"...and so you can see I have to be operating on all four cylinders if I want action," finished Kevin.

"Yes, er, it must take a lot out of you." She hadn't the faintest idea what he was talking about.

"You can say that again. That's why I need to relax in the evenings." He leered across the table. "Know what I mean?"

"I hope not," Selby began, but then their first course arrived, accompanied by waiters who flourished pepper grinders and plates of lemon, and generally put a stop to the conversation.

"Sure you won't change your mind and have oysters?" Kevin asked. She shook her head. "It's your loss. Personally I eat oysters whenever I get the chance. Great for the old sex drive!" He tipped one into his mouth and swallowed.

God, he was awful! What had she been thinking of when she'd accepted his invitation?

She pushed one of the tiny fried quail's eggs she'd ordered to one side, her appetite gone.

Kevin swallowed another oyster and said, "Hey! Isn't that old Danny? Over there by that clump of mums?"

"Is it?" she said, developing an intense interest in a black olive.

"Yeah! *He* didn't have any trouble getting a table by the window, I notice."

"This is *delicious*," Selby remarked brightly, nearly gagging on an egg.

"He's seen us," said Kevin, raising his hand in greeting.

She looked over and saw that Danny's table companion had leaned forward to see who was waving.

"That's a gorgeous babe he's with, I must say."

Must you? thought Selby in agony.

The woman was indeed gorgeous, with blond hair piled high, and great dark eyes, and Selby was overcome with such jealousy she nearly choked. She gave up all pretense of eating.

"He always gets the lookers," Kevin said, adding, "I can't think why. I mean, he's not that great looking himself."

"He looks all right," she said, thinking, *He looks a damn sight more attractive than you do, you oaf.*

More waiters arrived, presenting the turbot garnished with slices of sautéed bananas as if presenting debutantes at a ball, and Selby made all the right noises and dutifully ate some of the delicious fish, but she hardly tasted a thing.

The meal seemed to go on forever, even though she refused dessert and only drank one cup of coffee. While they were drinking this, Danny and his lady friend left the restaurant. She was even more lovely when she stood up. Willowy, and slim as the blade of a knife. Danny bestowed the most economical of nods when he passed their table, but the lovely blonde looked curiously at Selby, and Selby wondered if Danny had told her anything about their tempestuous non-affair.

She and Kevin left soon afterward, Kevin making a great to-do of helping her into her jacket, as if it were a sable wrap, and she realized that he'd had more than his share of the wine he'd ordered.

In the parking lot she turned to him. "Do you think you should drive, Kevin? We've had a lot of wine, and it's not far to my hotel."

His eyes lighted up. "You mean we should go back to your room?"

"I don't mean anything of the kind," she said crisply. "I'm simply suggesting that you sober up a bit before you drive."

"I'm perfectly sober," he said roughly, putting a hand on her arm, "and *I'm* suggesting that we drive back to my place and have a nightcap."

"I don't think so." She tried to shake his hand off. "Thank you for a lovely dinner... and good night."

"Come on, Selby! Live a little." His grip tightened. "You're too serious, y'know?"

"Don't be tiresome, Kevin," she said. "Don't spoil the evening."

"I'm not planning to *spoil* the evening," he said, leering. "I'm planning to make it better."

"Believe me, you're not going about it the right way," she said tartly.

He giggled drunkenly. "I love that icy British manner. It really turns me on."

"Well, you, Kevin, are turning me *off!*" she snapped.

"Aw, Selby!" He tried to kiss her, but she turned her mouth away so he only succeeded in grazing her lips. "Get off, Kevin! I'm not interested. Can't you understand?"

He fumbled at her, his hands hurting her now. "I could make you interested if you'd just relax."

"Listen to me, Kevin," she said clearly. "I'm saying no. Don't you understand? N. O. No!"

"Think you can just walk away after I bought you an expensive dinner—"

"I'll *pay* my share with pleasure, if it'll get rid of you," she fumed.

"Get rid of me! You bitch!" He grabbed clumsily at her waist and was attempting to haul her into the car when Danny came charging out of the shadows like an angry bull.

His voice cut through the dark like a steel blade. "Let her go, Kevin, before I break every bone in your body."

But he was too late. Selby had put to use those lessons she'd had on self-defense and Kevin was lying on the ground gasping with surprise.

CHAPTER TEN

"IS HE ALL RIGHT?" asked Selby anxiously.

"I hope not." Danny looked at her quizzically. "That's quite a trick."

"I took lessons."

"You must have been top of the class." Kevin pulled himself into a sitting position. "I wouldn't get up too soon if I were you," Danny advised him, "because if Selby's finished, I'm tempted to start on you myself. However, since I never hit a man when he's down, you're safer where you are."

Kevin glared at him. "I could have broken my back."

"You should learn to fall better, sonny boy, especially if you intend to continue carrying on like that. Haven't you heard? No means no, and women are learning to deal with creeps like you."

Selby said, "You asked for it, Kevin."

He scowled at her. "I could have you up for assault."

"And she could have *you* up for attempted rape," Danny pointed out, "so don't talk rubbish." He picked up Selby's purse and handed it to her. "Anything broken? If there is, lover boy here should replace it."

Kevin climbed to his feet, dusting off his trousers and ostentatiously examining them for tears. "It's nothing to do with you, Forest, but for your information, all I wanted was a good-night kiss, and this...this *maniac* starts throwing me around like I was attacking her."

Danny's nostrils pinched and flared dangerously. He said softly, "Don't add lies to the rest of your transgressions. I heard what was going on. You were after a great deal more than a good-night kiss."

"And what were you doing skulking around in the shadows spying on us?" Kevin demanded. "Are you after her yourself? Is that it? Well, be my guest. She's a cold fish, and expensive into the bargain—"

He would have gone on but he didn't get the chance, for Danny had grabbed him by his necktie and was squeezing the breath out of him. "You...filthy... little...scumbag," he snarled, shaking Kevin with each word, like a terrier shaking a rat. "You were a loathsome little creep at school, and you haven't changed."

"Lemme go!" whined Kevin, squirming in Danny's iron grip.

Selby, afraid Danny's temper would get the better of his good judgment, said, "Let him go. He's not worth this fuss."

"I guess you're right," said Danny, giving Kevin a final shake and throwing him against the side of his car. "Now get the hell out of here before I change my mind and pound the living daylights out of you."

"You haven't heard the end of this, Forest," Kevin said, straightening his tie.

"Don't push your luck," warned Danny, taking a step toward him.

Kevin climbed hastily into the car. "I'm going to complain to your father," he said through an inch of open window.

Danny smiled grimly. "You do that! I'm sure Dad'll be thrilled to find out what kind of trash he's employing."

"All this fuss over a stupid broad...."

But Danny had had enough. He kicked the side of Kevin's car, hard. "Get out of here before I wrench the damn door off," he said, and not waiting for more, Kevin put the car into gear and roared out of the parking lot.

"I don't think he's in any condition to drive," Selby said when his taillights had disappeared.

"Then let's hope he gets picked up by the cops." He looked at her coldly. "You don't care what happens to him, do you?"

"Of course not. But I don't want anyone killed."

"What got into you," he demanded, "going out with such a guy?"

"I met him at your parents' party," she said stiffly.

"That's no excuse." His face was a mask of careful indifference. "I know you can't stand the sight of me, but I can't say I find my replacement flattering."

She wanted to fling herself into his arms and reassure him that no one could ever replace him in her life. Instead, she mumbled, "He seemed fun at first."

Danny gave her a look that nearly singed her hair. "Well, all I can say is, you have a strange idea of fun."

"Anyway... thanks for coming to my rescue."

"It was unnecessary, wasn't it? You didn't need rescuing."

"I've learned to defend myself."

"If you're going to make a practice of going out with the likes of Kevin Talbot, you'll need to," he observed dryly.

"Well . . . good night." Except it really was "goodbye," because tomorrow she'd leave Halifax. She'd never see Danny again. She started to walk away, but he caught her by the arm.

"Where exactly do you think you're going?"

"Back to my hotel. It isn't far."

"You're not walking back alone in the dark, even if you are a female Rambo. I'll drive you."

"It's not *far*," she protested, because the longer she stayed in his company, the harder the inevitable parting.

He paid no attention. Tucking her arm into his, he walked her briskly toward a dove gray Mercedes.

"Anyway," she said, "what about your date? Don't you have to see her home?"

"My date?"

"The blonde you had dinner with."

"She went home ages ago." His gave a slight smile. "Back to her husband and son."

"Oh!"

"Too bad you saddled yourself with Kevin, otherwise you could have joined us."

She said bitterly, "I'm sure your friend would have liked that!"

"I'm sure she would have," he agreed, opening the door of the car for her. "She would have appreciated a female point of view."

Selby slid into the passenger seat. "About what?"

"About our business." He looked at her sardonically. "Willa's a senior partner in Scotia Trading."

"Oh!" The hand clenching Selby's heart loosened. She could breathe again.

"It was a business dinner, and Willa came in her own car." He climbed into the seat beside her. "Though why you should care is beyond me."

"I don't care. Of course I don't." Damn her expressive face. Maisy had always said if you wanted to know what Selby was thinking, all you had to do was look at her.

"Of course not. Now, where are you staying?"

She told him the name of her hotel. It really was just a few blocks away. A few blocks, and he would be out of her life forever. "I'm thinking of going to Ottawa tomorrow," she said, her voice sounding thin against the purr of the engine.

"I think you should put it off for a day," he said. "After all, you came to Canada to look up your grandmother's friend, didn't you? Not to go sightseeing."

"Gran's friend doesn't happen to be around, does he?" she muttered. "In fact, you could describe my whole trip as a fruitless journey."

Except that it wasn't true. Meeting Danny could never be described as fruitless. The rest of her life? Now that was another story.

He didn't speak until they'd drawn up in front of her hotel, then he said, "The object of your visit will be arriving back in this country tomorrow. My mother's gone hog-wild redecorating, so he'll be staying with me until the paint's dry. Why don't you come by in the afternoon, say around four, and meet him?"

At last she could accomplish what she'd come for—and she'd never felt more reluctant to grasp an opportunity. Life had taken such an unexpected turn that all her indignation on Maisy's behalf had disappeared.

"Oh, I don't know," she said. "He'll be tired after the flight...."

"Not too tired to meet you."

She was still reluctant. "If you're sure it won't be too much for him."

"You don't know my grandfather—he loves stimulation. Meeting the granddaughter of his old friend will really get rid of his jet lag."

It certainly would, but not for the reasons Danny imagined. "I'm not sure it's a good idea. Maybe I could write to him?"

"What about this promise you made to your grandmother when she was dying?"

"Well, I didn't exactly *promise* Gran," she confessed. "More myself, really."

He looked at her sharply. "You talked as if she'd asked about Granddad."

"She did." She'd cried out for him. Maisy, who had never cried out for anything in her life. "She . . . she talked about him a lot."

"Then you owe it to her, don't you?"

"Well—" she took a breath "—just a short visit."

"Short as you like," he said curtly. "Then at least you have done your duty."

He wrote his address on a page torn from the notebook in his pocket and handed it to her. For a second their fingers touched. The moment was as brief as the flicker of an eyelash, but she felt her fingertips tingle as if he had brushed her hand with fire.

"Tomorrow at four," he said. "We should be back from the airport by then."

Nodding, she climbed from the car, ridiculously disappointed because he didn't try to kiss her good night.

And why on earth should he, asked that small Maisy voice, *when you've done your level best to make him believe you don't like him?*

The following day she checked out of the hotel, booked an evening flight to Ottawa and left her luggage at the airport. By ten in the morning she had the rest of the day in front of her. It crawled by like molasses oozing out of a bottle. She couldn't settle to anything, and since she couldn't face lunch, she went to the Natural History Museum and looked at a lot of dinosaur bones. She wound up in a room designed to exhibit local marine life. The first exhibit her eye fell on was a small, short-billed bird with dark plumage. The mounted label in front of it read, DOVEKIE—EAST COAST ALCID—the bird she and Danny had gone to look for on their first disastrous date.

She stared at it mournfully. She had a suspicion she was going to stumble over reminders of Danny like this for the rest of her life. She would never be totally free of him, for no matter how deeply she buried his memory, he was in her very soul.

Not that she intended to mope for the rest of her life. She had her work, and there would be other men. Eventually she would marry one of them, raise a family—and go on quietly grieving inside for the rest of her life.

Well, she thought, a lot of women did that. A lot of women had successful lives, brought up children and had careers, in spite of having had the heart cut out of them by some unfortunate love affair. Maisy had done it, and she'd survived. *And I owe it to her to settle that debt. Then I can get on with the business of tearing Danny out of my heart and building my life again. And at least my pain won't be bitter; it won't be pain caused by treachery, the way Gran's was. And when Danny knows all the facts, he'll understand why there is no future for us, and he'll stop hating me. I can take some comfort in that.*

To stretch the time, she walked all the way to Danny's condominium, which was in a modern block built on a hill overlooking the harbor. Selby gave her name at the reception desk and looked around while the man phoned Danny's suite. Huge baskets of flowers stood on the polished parquet floor, and plump leather sofas were strategically placed next to low glass tables that held a few glossy magazines for guests to scan while they waited. Taste and luxury were as pervasive in the atmosphere as scent.

She was told that Mr. Forest was expecting her. "The penthouse, madam," said the desk clerk. "The far elevator's an express."

Going up in the elevator, she checked her appearance in the gold-flecked mirror. She looked a bit pale, but otherwise all right, her white blouse neat, her short beige skirt freshly pressed. The fact that she was bathed in cold quicksilver sweat and that her legs felt as if they belonged to somebody else didn't show, thank God.

Danny's front door was painted scarlet, like the door on the lighthouse, but there was no mermaid nailed to the shiny surface. She pressed the doorbell. A manservant answered, and Selby, who had been buoyed up to face Danny, stood at the entrance unable to speak.

The manservant asked, "Miss Maitland?" and then Barkis appeared, barking at the top of her lungs, her tail wagging a welcome.

"Hello, Barkis! Good girl," Selby choked out, overcome by this welcome. She put her arms around the dog's velvety beige neck and gave her a hug.

"She remembers you," said Danny, who had come into the hall. "Granddad and I only just got back from the airport. His plane was delayed. He's just freshening up. Come in. Robert'll make us tea."

Barkis was still weaving herself in and out of their legs, doing her best to trip them and uttering hoarse yelps of excitement.

"Take her into the kitchen, will you Robert?" Danny said. "Calm her down."

"She won't like it, sir," Robert said firmly. "She won't want to stay."

"Exercise your authority, man," Danny told him. "She's got you wrapped around her little paw."

"Yes, sir," he said, grabbing Barkis by the collar and dragging her away.

Selby and Danny were alone. He took her jacket and put it in the closet. While he did that, she examined her surroundings, but she was in no condition to take in very much. She had a blurred impression of highly polished floors, Swedish rugs, and a particularly lovely statue of a dolphin carved in marble.

"One of Lisa's," said Danny, "before she took to metal. This way."

He led her down two steps into the living room. Selby looked around slowly.

Light shimmered over white walls and bright pictures, over floors of dark polished wood strewn with rich Persian rugs and soft squashy sofas of buttery leather. At the far end of the room, floor-to-ceiling windows led to a balcony planted with trees and shrubs like a regular garden. A stand of slender-leafed dracaena plants stood against white silk curtains, adding to the general feeling of airiness. Below, she could see the harbor and glimpse container piers with the discreet lettering and logo of Scotia Trading over the entrance.

"Wow!" she said. "This is really something."

Danny came up behind her. "I take it you approve?"

"Who wouldn't? It's beautiful." And luxurious. She tried to conjure up a picture of Maisy's modest little house to rekindle her moral indignation, only it wasn't so easy to do anymore. "You seem to live permanently in the clouds," she said, thinking of the lighthouse.

"I come down to earth from time to time." He smiled.

Robert came in wheeling a tea trolley. "Your grandfather wants coffee, so I made a pot," he said, his lips thin with disapproval. "Although by rights he shouldn't be drinking caffeine at all."

"You should know by now that you can't tell Granddad what to do," Danny said. "If he wants coffee, he'll get it."

"Bad for his heart," grumbled Robert. "I made two kinds of tea—Earl Grey and English Breakfast."

"Thank you, Robert."

"And almond cookies and lemon bread."

"Thank you," said Danny, adding firmly, "We won't be needing you anymore, so you can go back to the football game. Just don't let Barkis out of the kitchen."

"Don't let the tea get cold," ordered Robert, "and don't let Mr. Forest drink too much coffee."

"He's been with the family for years," Danny explained when he'd gone. "He runs us."

Selby walked over to the windows again. "Old family retainers, old family business... You've got it all, haven't you?"

He looked at her, his obsidian eyes somber. "Not all. Just... *things*."

"Where I come from, this—" she made a sweeping gesture with her hand "—is *all*."

He caught her hands and held them, willing her to look up at him. "Does my being rich bother you, Selby? Is that why you constantly turn off me?"

She pulled her hands free. She couldn't be strong if he was touching her. "It's not your money," she said. "It's not that." She strode back into the center of the room, anxious to put distance between them. "You'll understand soon—when I've spoken to your grandfather."

He followed her. "Granddad? What's he got to do with us?"

"Please, Danny!" Her eyes were wide, imploring. "Please. Let it alone."

He bit his lips, then shrugged. "Anything you say. While we're waiting, let's have some of Robert's tea, shall we? He gets upset if I don't eat what he prepares."

"Will he be long? Your grandfather?" she asked, looking at her watch, and as if on cue, Daniel Forest came into the room.

He looked exactly like his grandson. The same black eyes, the same heart-melting smile. Only the thatch of silver hair and the lines in the angular face were different.

"Have I kept you waiting, Danny?" he asked. Even his voice had Danny's rich timbre. He looked appreciatively at Selby, standing tense as a coiled spring in front of him. "Not that you'd miss me when you've got such charming company." Danny made the formal introductions and the old man gestured toward the sofa. "Sit down, my dear, next to me. That grandson of mine can have your undivided attention later."

"Robert made you coffee, Granddad," Danny said. "Will you have some?"

"Damn right, I will!" his grandfather said.
"Wretched man gave me an argument." He glanced
over at Danny, who was pouring coffee into a delicate
porcelain cup. "I don't want my coffee in a thimble,
boy! Give me a proper mug."

"All the proper mugs are at the lighthouse," Danny
said. "You'll have to make do with a proper cup.
Selby? Earl Grey or English Breakfast?"

"I don't want any tea, thank you," said Selby, tight
as a rolled umbrella.

"Surely, my dear, just a cup! Pour her a cup,
Danny," said his grandfather. It was easy to tell where
Danny had inherited his autocratic ways.

Opening her purse, she fumbled for her papers. "I
understand you were in England during World War
Two, Mr. Forest."

Danny flashed her a quick look. "You sound like a
particularly zealous tax inspector, Selby," he said.

"That was a long time ago, my dear," said Mr.
Forest, taking a gulp of coffee and giving a sigh of
satisfaction. "Ah, that tastes good! Especially after
the swill they serve in England." He smiled at Selby.
"No offense, my dear, but English coffee does leave a
lot to be desired."

Selby, in no mood to discuss the merits of English
coffee, went on. "In point of fact, you were in London in 1942, weren't you?"

"You know damn well he was," Danny said.
"What's got into you?"

She ignored him and produced the photograph of
Maisy as a young woman. "Do you recognize the
woman in this picture?"

"What do you think this is?" protested Danny. "An audition for *L.A. Law*?"

Mr. Forest took the photo and squinted at it. "Can't really see well without my glasses," he said. "Pretty thing, though. I *can* see that."

She looked sternly into the old face that was so disconcertingly like Danny's. "You thought that in 1942, as well. That's a photograph of Maisy Tredwell."

Mr. Forest drew his brows together. "Tredwell... Tredwell... Doesn't ring a bell, I'm afraid."

Selby, strained to breaking point, turned on him savagely. "Oh, come *on*, Mr. Forest! You must remember her. You were close enough, God knows."

Danny said with ominous calm, "I think you must have overdosed on television, Selby. You're behaving like a character in a bad detective series." He turned to his grandfather. "Selby's grandmother died a few months ago, and Selby decided to look up her grandmother's old friend. At least—" he gave Selby a look that penetrated her very flesh "—that's what she said."

"I see." Mr. Forest peered at the photo again. "Sorry, my dear. I still can't place her. But it was a long time ago, and one met so many people...."

"Gran wasn't *people!*" blazed Selby, jumping to her feet. "She was your *mistress*. She loved you, and bore you a child...."

"*What!*" exclaimed Danny, rising and coming to one side of her.

"*What!*" echoed his grandfather, coming to the other.

"It's true," said Selby, feeling like the skimpy filling between two large slices of bread. "You're my—" she gulped on the word "—grandfather."

The beautiful room seemed to quiver in the silence that followed, then Mr. Forest said, "I assure you, my dear, I am not."

"So *that's* it," said Danny, looking at her through narrowed eyes. "Of course. That explains everything."

"It's no good denying it," said Selby heatedly. "Look! Here's my mother's birth certificate—dated nine months after you left for the front."

"That doesn't prove I was her father," Mr. Forest pointed out.

"And Gran told me she traced you after the war and you told her you were married, and you told her to get lost!" All Selby's former righteous anger was rekindled; she was riding on a tidal wave of ethical rage.

"Sit down, Selby," said Mr. Forest.

"I don't want to sit down."

"Sit *down*, dammit," Danny barked, and she collapsed back into her seat.

"You too, Danny," commanded the old man.

When the three of them were seated, he said, "I'm afraid, Selby, you've made a mistake. I never met your grandmother during the war or at any other time. You have been misinformed."

"If you mean that Gran lied to me, you're wrong," said Selby vehemently. "Gran never lied in her life."

"Not intentionally, I'm sure," Mr. Forest said. "But did she ever show you a photograph of me?"

"She didn't *have* a photograph of you," replied Selby bitterly. "You were too cagey for that. Besides, she didn't tell me about you until she was—'' Selby took a shuddering breath ''—until she was dying. Then she talked of nothing else.''

Mr. Forest said gently, ''You made a mistake, Selby. It's understandable. You were under a strain—''

''Don't patronize me,'' she flashed. ''I didn't make any mistake.''

''And how did you trace Granddad?'' asked Danny. ''There must be lots of Daniel Forests in Canada.'' His lip curled sardonically. ''Did you take a pin and make a stab at the *F*s in the phone book?''

She turned on him, slate eyes blazing. ''I hired a detective agency. Gran had said Danny Forest came from the East Coast of Canada, and it took a while, but they found him, and when they did I took the money Gran had left me and came to Canada.''

''You used the money she'd left you to come and find me?'' Danny's grandfather said wonderingly.

''I owed it to Gran,'' she said fiercely. ''All those years she brought me up, it was so hard for her. She had to struggle and skimp, and all that time you had all this—'' she waved her arm wildly at the window, at the distant container piers ''—and yet you never lifted a finger to help her.''

There was a silence following this outburst, then Danny said, his voice dangerously quiet, ''How much, Selby?''

''I don't understand,'' said Selby; but she did, and she went cold at the implication.

''Beth all over again, isn't it, Granddad?'' Danny went on. He sounded hideously chatty. ''We seem to attract scum like a stagnant pond.''

"Don't be too hasty, boy," his grandfather cautioned. He said to Selby, "You've made a mistake, Selby. I'm not saying it's deliberate—"

She cut in heatedly. "Don't try and wriggle out of it. Accept the blame, and preserve a bit of dignity."

"I can't accept the blame for something I didn't do," Mr. Forest said bluntly. So far, he had remained remarkably calm, but she sensed that his patience was wearing thin.

Danny's patience had worn out long since. "Stop this farce," he snarled at Selby. "I asked you a question. How much?"

"It isn't money I want," she said, but he wasn't listening.

"Just for the record," he went on, "what little sum came to mind when you'd done your assessment of this place? What kind of figure did you settle on?"

"I don't want any money," she cried, appalled that he had mistaken her admiration for an appraisal. "I just want an admission of guilt. An apology."

"If anybody deserves an apology around here, it's my grandfather," Danny said, his black eyes burning like coals. "Me, too, come to think of it."

"Let's not lose our tempers," said Mr. Forest. "Nothing will be gained by that." He looked suddenly very tired, and Selby felt a pang of guilt.

"All I owe you is an explanation, Danny," she said falteringly. "Just an explanation. You see, we're cousins, so now do you understand why I turned away from you?"

"Spare us more of your fabrications," Danny spat at her. "Don't think you can limp out of here like

Little Orphan Annie with a sizable check clutched in your greedy little hand.''

"Danny, *please*," she whimpered.

"Shut up," he commanded.

"Don't lose your temper, Danny," advised Mr. Forest.

Danny ignored him. "You were just weighing the options, weren't you, sweetheart?" he said to Selby. "Deciding if it was worth your while to marry for money, or to take what you could and run, and the immediate cash was more attractive than marriage to me, so you fended me off—"

"No, Danny. No!" She was crying now.

"Well, your little scheme just backfired," he said savagely. "On your feet!" He jumped up, hauling her out of her chair. "We don't have to listen to any more of your puerile lies." He thrust her purse into her hands. "On your way, lady, before I call the cops."

"Control yourself, Danny!" said his grandfather. "There's no need for this."

"I don't want any of your blasted money!" Selby yelled, but Danny wasn't listening. White with rage, he practically frog-marched her from the room.

"Your timing's off base," he said when they were at the front door. "Beth tried to blackmail the family ahead of you. You should have checked with her. She would have told you that we Forests don't take kindly to that sort of thing."

"I'm *not* trying to blackmail *anybody*," wailed Selby, but he had pushed her into the corridor outside. For the second time in seventy-two hours Danny shut the door in her face.

CHAPTER ELEVEN

SELBY FLEW BACK to England five days later. Her trip to Ottawa remained a blur, as did her visit to Niagara Falls, excursions taken to try to fill in the time before her flight home. But no matter how many art galleries she walked through or how many waterfalls she looked at, all she really saw was the blazing hatred in Danny's eyes.

She realized now that her scheme had been flawed from the start. Had she really believed that Maisy's lover would confess his guilt after fifty years? Had she really believed that a man of Daniel Forest's sophistication and background would beg forgiveness from his unknown—and unwanted—granddaughter?

She was filled with a dull sense of despair. She'd gone off on an ill-conceived quixotic vendetta. She'd failed Maisy, and now Danny despised her and thought she was a blackmailer. Terrific! Back at work she handed in her article on Savage Harbour. Her editor was pleased with the piece, but Selby could barely bring herself to look at it. It brought back too many memories, and memories were the things she wanted to abolish. To do this, she kept busy, taking on extra work, getting to the office before anyone else and leaving late, staggering back to the flat almost too tired to wash her face and fall into bed.

She had imagined she would lie sleepless at night remembering Danny and longing for him, but she was usually so exhausted she fell asleep the minute she crawled between the covers. However, most mornings she awoke to find her cheeks wet with tears. She couldn't remember the dreams that spawned them and didn't make any effort to do so. It was enough that the pain she carried around was like being stabbed with a blunt knife; she didn't need to search for the cause of her nocturnal weeping.

And so for six weeks life ground on, as gray and miserable as the weather. Then, late one evening, she stumbled home to find her flatmate, Kate, waiting for her in the hall.

"I've been trying to get you at the office," Kate hissed, "but the switchboard's closed."

Selby hung her raincoat in the closet. "What's the problem?"

"There's a man to see you." She pointed her chin in the direction of the sitting room. "Says his name's Danny Forest, *junior.* He was very insistent on the junior. He says he's *got* to see you, and he'll wait all night if necessary." She pulled a face. "Dishy bloke, but a proper bossy-boots."

"A tall man with a Canadian accent?" said Selby, who had started to shake, because this was both a dream *and* a nightmare come true.

"Tall and thin as a bean pole, but I thought the accent was American," said Kate. She looked at Selby, taking in the white face and trembling hands. "Is it someone you met on your holiday?" Selby nodded. "Is he why you've been so quiet lately? You might have told me."

"There didn't seem to be much point." She clasped her hands to try to stop their shaking. "I wonder what the hell he wants?"

Kate looked at her inquiringly. "Don't you want to see him?"

"No. Yes. I don't know." She pushed her hands through her damp curls. "I'd better go and see him, I suppose."

"Do you need moral support?" Kate asked. "It is my Polytechnic night, but I could stay here, if you'd rather."

Kate was obviously dying to stay, but Selby said firmly, "Of course you mustn't miss your class." She glanced at her watch. "It starts at eight, doesn't it? You're late already."

"If you're sure..."

"I'm sure. This won't take a minute, whatever it is. Now get a move on."

She left Kate pawing through the closet for her raincoat and made her way to the sitting room on legs that felt strangely heavy, so that walking was like wading through deep water.

Taking a deep breath, she opened the door. Danny was standing in front of the electric fire with his back toward her. When he turned she was shocked at how much older he looked, how sad, but in a second, like chalk wiped off a blackboard, the sadness was gone, to be replaced by that familiar mask of indifference.

"Hello, Selby," he said.

She took a faltering step into the room. "Wh-what are you doing here?"

He bared his teeth in a parody of a grin. "I'm here because I'm not all there."

"Please, Danny," she said, "I'm not up to bad jokes these days."

He hesitated and glanced in the direction of the hall. "Can we talk privately?"

"She's on her way out." Selby's head was spinning. Danny was in her sitting room. It wasn't a dream. He was real and warm and standing on the hearth rug, and part of her wanted to shout with joy, and part of her wanted to die.

"Would you like a drink?" she asked.

"No, thanks—" he blinked tiredly "—but I wouldn't mind a cup of coffee."

She went into the tiny kitchen, Danny following. "Did you just come from Canada?"

She sounded very unlike the Selby who'd chatted and laughed with him at Savage Harbour. But then, a lot had happened since Savage Harbour. Danny hadn't accused her of blackmail then.

"I flew in this morning. It seems like a long time ago," he said.

She couldn't bring herself to ask if he'd come simply to see her. First, because it was unlikely, and second, if he had, it was probably for an unpleasant reason. Like telling her the Forest family was laying charges or something.

"How did you find out where I lived?" she asked, holding the kettle under the tap, surprised she was managing to hold it steady.

"Your office." He gave her another ghastly grin. "Security doesn't seem to be a priority at your place of work. They gave me your address without a murmur."

"I'll have to speak to them," she said, brittle as an eggshell.

Kate called, "'Bye now!" and the front door slammed.

An unnatural quiet fell. Selby clutched the tin of coffee to her breast, as if the reality of it could give her comfort.

"It's only instant, I'm afraid," she babbled. "Kate and I can't be bothered with real coffee. It's awful of us, I know, but there's no time in the mornings, and at night we're so tired, what with work... and then Kate takes evening classes—"

"Shut up about the damn coffee and put the kettle on!" he snapped. "You're making my head spin."

She did as ordered. "Too bad travel doesn't improve your temper." His sudden irritability was like a hand brushing away a cobweb. This was the Danny she recognized, not that sad, withdrawn stranger. The inhibiting tension was eased and she went on crisply, "Suppose you tell me why you're here? I'm not good at guessing games."

He answered wearily, "I've been asking myself the same question ever since I arrived. However, I do have something to tell you."

"Something else?" she said, with a blazing look.

"Come back in here," he said, and she followed him into the sitting room. He picked up his briefcase and took out a sheet of paper. "You left this behind.'' He handed it to her, and she saw it was the report from the detective agency she'd hired to find Daniel Forest. ''I did some checking,'' said Danny, ''which, I'll bet, is more than you did. Checking things out isn't exactly your line, is it?''

She colored painfully, and remained silent.

''What on earth made you choose that particular agency, Selby? To say that their reputation stinks is putting it charitably.''

Her pale cheeks flushed deeper. ''I looked them up in the phone book. I mean, I don't go around hiring detectives every day of the week. That seemed the simplest way.''

The skin around his eyes looked bruised with fatigue. ''Did you know that there's an organization here in England set up expressly to trace the fathers of children sired by American and Canadian servicemen during World War Two?'' She shook her head. ''No. You just went off half-cocked, didn't you? Impulsively. Not stopping to think.''

''Did you come all the way across the Atlantic to lecture me?'' she asked. ''Because it's not necessary. I'm sorry I caused you trouble. In fact—'' she swallowed a lump the size of a golf ball ''—I'm sorry I ever even heard about the Forest family. But you needn't panic. I don't plan to bother you again.''

''What am I supposed to say?'' he asked tartly. ''Thanks, and ask for a sworn affidavit that you'll never visit Canada?''

She burst out passionately, ''What the hell do you want, Danny? Do you want me to crawl, is that it?

Well, I'm not the crawling kind, so would you please get the lecture over with and leave me in peace."

"I didn't come to lecture you," he said, and if her eyes hadn't been masked in tears she would have seen that his were tender. "I came to give you some information." He went into the briefcase again and took out another document. "I got in touch with War Babes—that's the organization I mentioned—and they traced your grandfather. Your *real* grandfather."

She looked up at him swiftly. "You mean . . . ?"

"First, you got the spelling wrong. Your grandfather's surname was spelled with two *r*'s—F-o-r-r-e-s-t."

"Are . . . are you sure?" she asked, rattled.

"I'm quite sure. I talked to the family."

"And do they—does he—live in Halifax, too?"

"No. He never did. Did your grandmother actually mention Halifax by name?"

She searched in her memory. "She said . . . the East Coast of Canada. That's what I told the detective agency, and they traced him to Halifax."

"And the spelling of the name? Did she spell his name for you?"

"No," she admitted. "I just assumed—"

"Oh, Selby, Selby!" He shook his head in despair.

"And my . . . my *real* grandfather, where does he live?"

"He died ten years ago. He lived in a place called Durham, in New Brunswick."

"So I was chasing a ghost." She gave a sad little chuckle. "Do you know any more about him?"

"Not much. He was married before the war and had three children, two of whom are still living but have moved out of the province. His wife knew all about your grandmother, but she's an old lady now and she's not anxious to dig up her late husband's murky past. She never was." He put the paper into her nerveless fingers. "Here! It's yours. In case you want to contact your relations."

"No," she said. "There's no point anymore."

"You mustn't blame yourself, Selby," said Danny softly. "You did it because you loved her."

"Yes." But Maisy wouldn't have wanted revenge. Selby saw that now. She'd been so shattered by her grandmother's death that she'd used her pity for Maisy, her outrage, as a shield against grief.

As if he could read her thoughts, Danny said, "It's time to let her go, Selby. Let her rest in peace."

She nodded. "Yes," she said, knowing that her mourning would no longer be corroded by bitterness, that a great weight had been rolled off her heart.

"What is it that's screaming like a hedgehog in a rage?" Danny asked, and she came back to earth with a bump.

"Oh, my God!" she cried, rushing into the kitchen, where the whistling kettle was shrieking for attention. "I forgot about your coffee!"

He came up behind her and turned off the gas, and the kettle died with a hiss.

"Forget the coffee, Selby," he said quietly. "It's not what I need."

His mouth claimed hers and she gave a little choking sob and clung to him, oblivious of time and space, conscious only of the warmth of his lips, the taste of him, the scent of his flesh. . . .

After a while he stopped kissing her, but he still held her close, as if fearful she would disappear. "It nearly killed me when you kept drawing away from me," he said huskily.

"I thought we were related," she said. "Closely related. It nearly killed me, too."

"Oh, my love!"

She wound her arms around his waist and held him tight, as if to prove to herself this was not a dream.

He kissed her on the bridge of her nose and then on each eyelid before saying, "Do you think we could go and sit down? I hate to be unromantic, but it's been a long day."

"Of course." She laughed shakily. "I'm not sure I can stand up much longer myself."

Sitting on the sofa, they continued to hold each other close, unable to be apart for a moment. He stroked her hair. "I've ached for you," he murmured, "until I thought I was going to die. Everything I see or hear or touch speaks to me of you."

"Even when you thought I was blackmailing you?"

"Even then." He gave a ragged sigh. "Oh, Selby, sweetheart, I'm so sorry. I've been a bit...a bit crazed. Those things I said—I didn't really believe them. I was thinking of someone else."

"Of Beth?"

He nodded. "Of Beth, and God knows I *must* have been crazed, because there couldn't be two women less alike."

"What did she do to you, for heaven's sake?"

"She altered a letter I'd written to make it look like a proposal of marriage, then she threatened to sue for breach of promise. She said she'd drag the family through the mud unless I agreed to a wedding. But it wasn't a wedding she wanted—she wanted a nice fat settlement. She couldn't wait to get her hands on the Forest money. When I threatened to call in the police, she left town in a hurry. I found out later that she'd tried a similar scam in Vancouver." His mouth twisted ruefully. "She took me in completely at the beginning. It wasn't until she produced that doctored letter that I realized I was being taken for a ride."

"And you thought I wanted your money, too?"

"I don't know what I thought. But when you kept turning away from me... I couldn't understand why you didn't simply go on...dazzling me, because that's what you do, my love. If money was what you wanted, I would have given it to you. I would have given you anything you wanted. So then I thought—she must really dislike me, and even though there's this overwhelming sexual attraction between us, she can't bring herself to accept it." He looked haggard, the strain of the past weeks etched on his face. "It drove me insane."

"I turned away because I thought you were my cousin," she said, and then she asked, because she *had* to know, "Beth... Was she beautiful?"

"She was beautiful. Yes."

For an instant she hated him, but only for an instant. "You were lovers?"

"Briefly. But it was never serious, and I never led her to believe that it was." He tilted her chin and looked into her gray eyes. "I won't lie to you. There have been women in my life."

"Yes, that's what Lori said. She said you were attractive to women." She felt that unfamiliar stab of jealousy again.

"Lori exaggerates. Besides, I'm not interested in *women*, I'm only interested in one woman." He put his fingers beneath her chin to turn up her face. "I don't know if you've noticed, Selby Maitland, but I'm more than a little interested in you."

But she was in no mood for teasing. "Gran fell for a man who was attractive to women," she said, "and she never got over him."

He smoothed back an unruly curl that had fallen over her brow. "If I thought you could never get over me," he said softly, "I'd be the happiest man in the world, because you see, sweetheart, I'm nuts about you, and I plan to stay that way for the rest of my life."

That was wonderful—but she had to be sure. "That's really projecting into the future."

"I can't afford to lose you," he said, his expression haunted. "I know you're the only woman for me, and I can't spend the rest of my life going around like a zombie without you."

She gave a shaky little giggle. "I do know what you mean."

He caressed the back of her neck. Electric currents started running deliciously up and down her spine. "Is it too soon to ask you to marry me, Selby?"

The room seemed suddenly radiant with light, but she was learning not to give in to impulse, even when it was all she wanted in the world. "But your family... How will they take it?"

"It's *me* you'd be marrying," he said, "but my family's not a problem. Mom likes you, Dad will come around to the idea, and Granddad would adore to have you as a granddaughter-in-law."

"I find that hard to believe."

"It's the truth. He fell for you in spite of all the nasty things you called him. He thinks you've got character."

"I'm not sure about that. I seem to have made a right mess of things up to now."

"I wouldn't say that," Danny murmured. "After all, you're not exactly drawing away from me at the moment."

"That's true," she said, snuggling closer. "And if I married you, I wouldn't have to go to detectives to find out who my relatives are."

"Now *that* is thinking rationally," he agreed, and then he started kissing her again.

Let

HARLEQUIN ROMANCE®

take you

BACK TO THE

Come to Bluebonnet Ranch,
in the Hill Country of Texas!

Meet Olivia Faraday, quintessential New Yorker. *And*
Lucas Chance, one sexy cowboy. It's city versus
country! It's East versus West. Will even a state the
size of *Texas* be big enough for the two of them?

Read COUNTERFEIT COWGIRL
by Heather Allison,
our April Back to the Ranch title!

Available wherever Harlequin books are sold.

Take 4 bestselling love stories FREE

Plus get a FREE surprise gift!

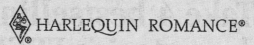
HARLEQUIN ROMANCE®

Question: **What will excite & delight Debbie Macomber's fans?**
Answer: A sequel to her popular 1993 novel,
READY FOR ROMANCE!

Last year you met the two Dryden brothers, Damian and Evan, in
Debbie Macomber's READY FOR ROMANCE. You saw Damian fall in
love with Jessica Kellerman....

Next month watch what happens when Evan discovers that
Mary Jo Summerhill —the love of his life, the woman who'd
rejected him three years before—*isn't* married, after all!

Watch for READY FOR MARRIAGE: Harlequin Romance #3307
available in April wherever Harlequin books are sold

When the only time you have for yourself is...

Spring into spring—by giving yourself a March Break! Take a few *stolen moments* and treat yourself to a Great Escape. Relax with one of our brand-new stories (or with all six!).

Each STOLEN MOMENTS title in our Great Escapes collection is a complete and never-before-published *short* novel. These contemporary romances are 96 pages long—the perfect length for the busy woman of the nineties!

Look for Great Escapes in our Stolen Moments display this March!

SIZZLE by Jennifer Crusie
ANNIVERSARY WALTZ
by Anne Marie Duquette
MAGGIE AND HER COLONEL
by Merline Lovelace
PRAIRIE SUMMER by Alina Roberts
THE SUGAR CUP by Annie Sims
LOVE ME NOT by Barbara Stewart

Wherever Harlequin and Silhouette books are sold.

HARLEQUIN®

Don't miss these Harlequin favorites by some of our most distin-
guished authors!
And now, you can receive a discount by ordering two or more titles!

Harlequin Promotional Titles

          (short-story collection featuring Anne Stuart, Judith Arnold,
          Anne McAllister, Linda Randall Wisdom)
(limited quantities available on certain titles)

	AMOUNT	$	
DEDUCT:	10% DISCOUNT FOR 2+ BOOKS	$	
ADD:	POSTAGE & HANDLING	$	
	($1.00 for one book, 50¢ for each additional!)		
	APPLICABLE TAXES*	$ _____	
	TOTAL PAYABLE	$ _____	
	(check or money order—please do not send cash)		

To order, complete this form and send it, along with a check or money order for the
total above, payable to Harlequin Books, to: **In the U.S.:** 3010 Walden Avenue,
P.O. Box 9047, Buffalo, NY 14269-9047; **In Canada:** P.O. Box 613, Fort Erie, Ontario,
L2A 5X3.

Name: _____

Address: _____ City: _____

State/Prov.: _____ Zip/Postal Code: _____

*New York residents remit applicable sales taxes.
  Canadian residents remit applicable GST and provincial taxes.
                                      HBACK-JM